Praise for This

Readers will fall hard for sweet M____ ____
funerals. At first, her misadventures at The Peaceful Rest make it hard for this
new employee to urn her new job....but it's not long before she's digging up
buried clues and making a difference in her small town. Many bouquets of
flowers to Carole Lynn Jones for creating these stories.

~Nancy Martin, author of the *Blackbird Sisters Mysteries*

Fast-paced and rollickingly hilarious, This New Job's Murder will keep you
chuckling and turning the page from beginning to end. Only a comedic talent
could make working in a funeral home so much fun!

~Annette Dashofy, USA Today Bestselling Author of the *Zoe Chambers*
Mystery Series

Fresh from an unexpected break-up, former paralegal and plucky vintage
clothing fashionista Melody Shore undertakes a new job at the Peaceful Rest
Funeral Home and Cemetery, turning her don't quit attitude and mad legal
admin skills to solve five twisty mysteries. Packed with laugh-out-loud humor,
a heartfelt hometown setting, and an intriguing new romance, Melody proves
that with the right accessories, anything is possible.

~Martha Reed, author of *Love Power,* a Crescent City NOLA Mystery
& 2021 Killer Nashville Silver Falchion Award Winner

Think working in a funeral home is deadly dull? Think again. Melody
Shore has the smarts to solve any puzzle—and the vintage couture to look good
doing it.

~Liz Milliron, author of *The Laurel Highlands Mysteries* and *The*
Homefront Mysteries

Melody Shore is back in her quaint hometown and working at the local
funeral home, but there's more in those caskets than dead bodies. In her vintage
heels, she stumbles upon secrets and unravels crimes. If you like a lighthearted
romp with quirky comedic characters, you'll fall in love with all the residents of
Pleasantville.

~Tina deBellegarde, Agatha and Derringer-nominated author of the
Batavia-on-Hudson Mystery Series

This *New Job's* Murder

The Melody Shore Mysteries

by

Carole Lynn Jones

FLYING KETCHUP PRESS ®

Kansas City, Missouri

All inquiries should be addressed to:

    Flying Ketchup Press
    11608 N. Charlotte Street,
    Kansas City, MO 64155

Library of Congress Cataloging-Publication Data
This New Job's Murder: The Melody Shore Mysteries / Carole Lynn Jones
Library of Congress Control Number: 2022936464
Softcover ISBN-13: 9781970151-39-8
ePub ISBN-13: 9781970151-41-1

☙

To Jimmy ~ Every reason, all seasons, and my lifetime

This New Job's Murder

Carole Lynn Jones

❦

Contents

One look into the closet did nothing for my mood. Seven wrinkly white blouses and pencil skirts that my post-breakup eating had made too small. But I wasn't going to back down. My favorite T-shirt says, "Not a Mashed Potato." It's true...

The Right Accessory for Murder

S ome people say they talk to the dead. I don't profess to be a medium, but I do spend a lot of time with the deceased.

"We got it!" J.J. said. He slid out the nameplate on my desk, and replaced it with my name, "MELODY SHORE."

Handing off "REGINA SNUGG" to his twin brother, Alex grabbed the nameplate, then made an exaggerated basketball shot into the garbage can. "Swish, dunk, game over," Alex said.

"Sorry, not sorry, Aunt Regina," J.J. added. He snapped the gum in his mouth, adjusted his man bun and plopped his lanky six-foot frame down into my spare office chair.

"Won't you miss your aunt?" I asked, pushing my new vintage tortoise-shell glasses a little higher on my face.

"Aunt Regina, the Army Sergeant? No…" Alex began. "Uncle Arthur might though, I guess."

"It's not all bad. He got the funeral home in the divorce," J.J. pointed out.

"Not true! It was his already!" Alex grabbed some paper and crumpled it into a ball. "His grandpa's, then his dad's, now his."

J.J. shrugged, grabbed Alex's paper ball and shot it into the garbage can.

"Why did you even want to work here anyway, Melody?" Alex asked. "Don't get us wrong, we're glad you're here, but—"

"You're kinda overqualified," the boys announced together.

"My dad—" I polished my name plate a bit and waited so my voice wouldn't choke. "He used to be Snugg's business partner before he died. I used to work at this legal office in Pittsburgh. But you know with the stock market slide they had cutbacks."

What I couldn't tell them? At twenty-eight, with a Mazda RX8 one inspection short of the scrap pile, and college debt looming over my head, I left my career to move back home. The deciding factor for leaving was my double patio doors that faced my ex-boyfriend's condo. It wasn't that he and his new girlfriend liked to spend all their free time on their deck cooking out and drinking wine. It was that I couldn't solve the mystery of why he didn't "grill" or "drink wine" when we lived together.

"I just couldn't stay there," I said to the twins. "I loaded up Clifford, my red Mazda, and drove back here to Pleasantview. Only two hours away, and suddenly I was back home." No boyfriend, no job, and no prospects, I added to myself.

"But why here?" Alex prodded.

"Well, now that you mention it, my car was dead on arrival, and I can take the bus here from my new apartment. You know?" I smiled broadly.

"Ah." The twins nodded but with confused frowns.

"You two are next then."

"To die?" J.J. asked in horror.

"No, I mean you are next in line to own The Peaceful Rest."

"Um, no. What makes you think we want to inherit this old place? I mean, what if we wanted to go pro basketball, or become Olympians?" J.J. said.

"Wow, I didn't know you two were such athletes."

"This weekend we will be." J.J. pulled a folded piece of paper out of his pocket and tossed it on my desk, posing chest out, hands on his hips, like receiving a gold medal.

It was an advertisement for the "Beer Olympics."

APPLY TODAY!! We're looking for the best beer guzzlers in Charles County. Only twenty dollars to enter. Cash prize of $5000 for first place. Present this flyer and receive a prize pack cooler. No entries accepted after five p.m.

"Alex, J.J. The Lilac Room. NOW!" Arthur Snugg hollered from the foyer.

"Saved by Uncle Arthur," I muttered under my breath. I sank into the chair J.J. had finally vacated and eased my feet out of my 1940 Mary Jane pumps. I love vintage, but it doesn't always love me.

While Snugg chewed out the twins for something in the Lilac Room, I sorted through yesterday's mail. The Lilac Room is the smaller of The Peaceful Rest's two viewing rooms, and unlike the Rose Room, it is more modern. Its tan carpet blends into the violet walls and a wallpaper of tiny purple lilacs, intermixed with splotches of tan and gray.

I removed Regina Snugg's nameplate from the garbage and placed it in a box that I filled with her angel statues, a personalized stationery set, coffee mugs, costume jewelry, and two monogrammed black sweaters. Apparently, she no longer had a use for anything labeled "RS."

Snugg emerged quickly from the "meeting" with the twins and marched into my fishbowl-sized office. His jet-black hair matched his high-gloss shoes and pinstripe suit. His tie choice—a pattern of goldfish—taunted me.

"You have a date, Mr. Snugg? You look especially nice today," I said.

"Melody, about tonight." He placed a folder in my hands.

"Ella Sandstrom's first viewing, right?"

"Correct."

"I will take care of it, sir." Before he could stop me, I stapled and alphabetized the documents into a neat pile and printed a label for her file. "Let's see, we have the death certificate—I'll file for duplicates—life insurance claim, memorial service info, cost sheet copy, burial plot map, obituary text, and copy…Everything seems to be here." I peered over my tortoiseshell glasses, but Snugg's attention was on me, not the folder.

"He was top-notch, my right hand…" Snugg smiled a rare dour smile, but it quickly faded. "Your dad was, I mean."

"I miss him too." I glanced at the Rose viewing room where his casket had been when I was sixteen.

"When you came in here three weeks ago soaking wet with an inside-out umbrella and asked me to hire you, I was apprehensive."

"I'm still sorry about knocking over that peace lily, Mr. Snugg."

"Nonsense. You've proved yourself, Melody."

"I appreciate you saying that, Mr. Snugg. I think Dad would be happy, too." I hadn't told him about the rainbow I saw on that first day. Just out near the far perimeter of the cemetery. That was between Dad and I.

"And, if you continue to excel, I will consider expanding your job duties. Your schooling and your office skills warrant that," Snugg said with a curt nod.

"That would be great!" I jumped up and staved off the impulse to make more labels, random ones with my name on them. Instead, I held out my hand to shake on the promise. "Wait…no dead body stuff, right?" I had a sudden horrible vision of myself holding tubes filled with embalming fluid.

"No, I'm the one who went to school for that, Melody."

"Woot! I mean—You're welcome, Mr. Snugg, and thanks."

"Now, tonight is the first viewing, and remember, because of the family stature, a second viewing will be tomorrow evening. Burial is on Saturday."

"Got it." I sat back down, peeked at my reflection in the office glass, and fluffed my light brown curls. Then it hit me. "Wait. Mr. Snugg, you sound like you aren't going to be here."

"Tonight, will be your night to handle. I have plans I cannot reschedule." Snugg straightened his tie and buttoned his suit coat to leave.

"I've only been here three weeks!" My voice was a mere squeak, and my hands scattered the stacks of neatly organized files piled on my desk.

"Melody. Simply open the doors, greet the family, and offer any support they need."

"What if there's a problem?"

"I'm sure there won't be. But if you have questions, I will address them in the morning."

"What about Alex and J.J.?"

"They are leaving after Harriet Carter's burial this afternoon. They asked for time off to attend something called the Beer Olympics…? I'm hoping I didn't hear that right."

I walked him out past the Lilac and Rose Rooms, and past the mahogany staircase with the ornate wooden banister that led to his office.

"It's actually a lot easier without them here. They don't know yet, but I'm cutting their hours. I can't keep paying them for playing foosball in the basement—which reminds me, have them clean their office on Monday. It looks like a college dorm room, maybe worse."

"I understand, Mr. Snugg," I said, holding the door. "I'll take care of everything."

"Hmm…and, Melody, please remember to wear something appropriate."

"What's wrong with my dress?" I shouted from the porch. I looked down at my orange cocktail dress circa 1963 and red Mary Janes with white bows, but Mr. Snugg was halfway to his car. Maybe this combination was overkill for a viewing.

As I headed back inside, I saw Alex and J.J. on the east lawn. Riding in the tractor with a trailer hitched behind holding the Harriet Carter casket, they sped along at full throttle. Harriet was an elderly woman sent by the Pine Creek Nursing Home because of her last wish for a "proper" burial. I couldn't see how her wish would ever be met with Alex and J.J. on the job. They drove down the path, past the incinerator, and stopped to fill the trailer with broken wooden crates. My heart dropped to my stomach. I couldn't understand it. Were they going to build a funeral pyre? I didn't dare breathe until they dropped off the scrap wood with some brush for the burn pile and turned around to drive the body out to the cemetery.

When they finally stopped safely at the gravesite, I sighed with relief. Then I realized they were doing two chores at once so they could leave early. Why didn't I think of that first?

The weather was spring-like, but when I returned home for a quick dinner, my apartment walls were as white as January. I only had two hours to get back to work, but I couldn't stop reorganizing the framed photos I had lying all over the floor. Sure, they aren't all that. I took them myself... took them with my dad. Why can't I stop thinking about him today? Probably because he gave me my first camera for a birthday gift. I was maybe ten...?

***

"Most people don't know Pittsburgh is the city of bridges," Dad said as we were planning a photo shoot day trip after my birthday. It was a Saturday, and we were about to jump in his old Ford Ranger to go find our ten top favorites.

"Which one do you like the best?" he asked, tugging my ponytail.

"Can we go to all of them today, Daddy?"

"Well, kiddo, we can die trying."

***

Dad was such a jokester. I never appreciated his humor until now. I wound the dial on my butterfly wristwatch. It was getting late. I needed to get ready and none of the photo arrangements I laid out seemed right. Finally, I placed them back in a box. When I got paid, I would buy a shelf and some end tables. Ironic. I had worked so hard: I'd left home after high school, earned my paralegal degree, met a guy I thought was the perfect partner, and climbed the corporate ladder. Now here I am back where I started with every bridge in my life burned. I always say the stock market was the reason I lost my job, but Thomas & Davis fired me for "noticing" they overbilled their clients. Well, actually, I had also sent the clients' statements showing the billing issues. My ex-employer, like my ex-boyfriend, really believed in screwing others.

Shaking off my mental gloom, I headed to the bedroom. One look into the closet did nothing for my mood. Seven wrinkly white blouses and pencil skirts that my post-breakup eating had made too small. But I wasn't going to back down. As my favorite T-shirt says, "Not a Mashed Potato," I'm a stand-up citizen. The reason I'm here in this tiny apartment—about to go hang out with dead people—is because I don't lay down in a lump and let people walk all over me. I will be a great hostess or die trying. Well, maybe not literally.

I pulled out a burnt orange cardigan and looked in the mirror. It wouldn't do for tonight. My mother gave it to me. I had only stayed with her one night when I arrived. That's all I could really handle. The next day I drove around until I saw a "For Rent" sign on an apartment above a garage on Pine Street. I guess you could call it a carriage house, but anything is better than living with my mother again. Right away her presence started suffocating me.

***

"So, is there any chance of a reconciliation with Grant?" my mother asked as she watched me unload the last of the boxes from my car.

"Oof," I groaned as I lifted box seventeen out of Clifford with beads of perspiration soaking through my 1935 look-alike, art deco blouse with Dolman sleeves. I knew this wasn't the right choice for moving day, but some styles are too good to save for special occasions. "No, Mom, there isn't," I answered.

"Perfect, because there's a new cook at Marsha's. I've already arranged for you two to meet." She opened the box marked "bathroom" and proceeded to rifle through it.

***

I stopped getting ready for work and turned on some tunes. My favorite playlist ran loud enough to drown out the memories I didn't want to think about. In the fridge, I pulled out takeout from Marsha's Café down on Eighth Street. Marsha is my mom's closest friend. She stocked me up with a few hot meals. The smell of her homestyle turkey sandwich on homemade bread and fresh green beans made my stomach growl in approval.

I looked at my watch. Only twenty minutes to dress and catch the bus back to work.

Back in my closet, I peeled through fifteen vintage outfits I'd collected. They ranged from an authentic poodle skirt to a color-blocked number with go-go boots. Pretty sure none of those are what Snugg had in mind.

Finally, there is nothing left but one dress bag in the back closet. It's the dress from that night. The one I've been trying not to remember for a month now. I gathered the black dress out of the garment bag; its sleeveless ruched bodice with lace at the yoke had ruffles down the side.

***

My boyfriend Grant and I walked into Anastasia's, the fanciest restaurant in our neighborhood. It was our four-year anniversary. Only one day away from Valentine's Day, I knew this was my lucky night. My attention was split between the pasta carbonara, the homemade cannoli, and the fact that I picked out the perfect dress for the marriage proposal I knew was coming.

Still chewing a huge bite of steak, Grant said, "Melody, by looking at you tonight, I can see you for who you really are."

"Wow. Thanks, Grant," I gushed. Grant wasn't often spendy with his words. "I knew you would like this dress. It's a totally authentic Mignon from 1960 with handmade lace…"

"Oh no, sweetheart. I wanted this night to celebrate us and tell you I want to give you the freedom you've been hinting about."

"Grant," I said, my stomach instantly in knots and the wine going straight to my head.

"I mean, I know you've been wanting to date other people, Melody. That's what this night is about."

"I haven't been hinting about breaking up. I've been hinting at getting en…"

"…enough time to move out. Yes, I knew that, so I already let the landlord know I will be moving next week. Let's toast. To us."

"Are you serious right now?" My voice was getting loud.

"Melody, let's be real. We don't belong together. Look at what you're wearing tonight. For one, you look like you are about to go to a funeral. Second, I'm wearing a football jersey. Why can't you just be normal like everyone else? Why do you spend all your time and cash hunting down your stupid vintage whatevers? Would it have hurt you to just wear a halter top and jeans like every other girl?"

***

Poor Grant. He hadn't even noticed that it was a black-tie restaurant. He was the one who stood out. Memories or no memories, I had no other choice. I wanted to burn the dress, but Grant had been right about one thing: it was really going to be good for a funeral, a serious improvement from spending one more minute with that jerk.

I put on the dress. "Not a mashed potato!" I said into the mirror.

Feeling the need for a confidence boost, I texted Claire. She is the one good friend I have reconnected with since I returned home. She owns Claire's Cottage on Fifth Street, a resale shop brimming with beautiful treasures and vintage clothing. Claire is taller than I am with high cheekbones that won't quit and piercing blue eyes. Now that I'm back, we have an agreement: I give her my no-longer-loved clothing, and she gives me store credit to purchase something that I cannot live without.

Me:	Accessory advice for black lace boatneck dress?
Claire:	Umm…Are u okay? Who died?
Me:	No one. I mean one person. For work. First night in charge.
Claire:	Creepy work event. But why are u sad?
Me:	Black dress from you know who is all I have to wear to work!!
Claire:	Why didn't you get a dress when u were here Saturday? I'll bring you one tomorrow. Diamond stud earrings.

Breakfast at Tiffany's. Do you even have to ask?
Me: Thanks. TTYL.

I twisted my hair up into a tight bun and put on the earrings. Then, I ran to the bus stop and just made it.

I arrived in sight of The Peaceful Rest right on time. Republic Street darkened as large raindrops fell. After traversing the wet asphalt parking lot in my heels, I climbed the steps to the wraparound porch. For a few minutes, I leaned against the Queen Anne sandstone, looking out toward the cemetery. The many headstones stared back soundlessly, like they were listening to my rapid breathing. I imagined their gossip to each other that I should have spent more time in yoga so my dress still fit and that I probably couldn't handle tonight on my own. That made me more determined. I saluted the stones and marched through the funeral home doors.

Inside, quiet music played just as I'd left it. The lights were still on and Ella Sandstrom was laid out in the Rose Room. A quick look reassured me everything was ready. Flower baskets sat to the left and right of her casket, and roses draped the top. Wingback chairs framed the walls, and the dark cherry coffee tables had full mint dishes and fresh boxes of tissues on them. I took a butter mint from the dish and stole a quick look at the deceased. I was getting used to being around dead bodies. It's not so bad. She looked peaceful. I hummed softly as I turned on the two crystal floor lamps that stood on either side of her casket. They cast dim shadows on the tiny rosebud covered wallpaper.

I was standing in the lobby, eating another mint when David Sandstrom, husband of the deceased, and a modest group of family and friends arrived.

"Good evening, Mr. Sandstrom. Melody Shore. If I can assist you in any way, please let me know."

He ran his hand across his perfectly combed hair, buttoned the jacket of his impeccable suit, and then turned to me. His black eyes were dark. "Thank you," was all he said.

I retreated to my office for fifteen minutes. Though they could see through the walls, I feel it gives the family privacy. Heading back in with the prayer cards and a guest book, I entered the Rose Room, now full of mourners. A couple more must have slipped in when I wasn't looking.

My first observation—I shouldn't have worn the dress.

About twenty people occupied the room. A few men stopped talking and stared. Several women whispered and grabbed the arms of their men. I looked down to see if something was off. The material that used to cling slightly to my breasts and show a hint of cleavage was now tightly stretched, threatening fairly serious exposure.

That's when the screaming started.

Standing at the casket, David Sandstrom yelled, wielding his cane in outrage like a studio wrestler swinging a folding chair in the ring.

Most of the attendees backed out of the room. Several ran out the door.

An older woman in a red suit walked straight up to Mr. Sandstrom. His cane circled wildly above her head, but with incredible strength for a woman her size, she grasped his arms and pinned them behind his back.

I recognized Frances Blooming from her commercials on the local cable channel. Dressed in a tulip red, flutter cuff silk blouse, boot cut black pants, and black wedge sandals, she was stunning for someone well over sixty. She was a walking advertisement for health, wealth, and beauty for seniors.

"David, what is wrong?" she asked.

"These are not her jewels! These are not my wife's jewels!" He stomped his feet.

The jewels displayed on Ella Sandstrom were diamonds of varying sizes, which hung from her ears and neck. A large diamond was mounted in the necklace center.

While I loved jewelry, I only knew the basics. But, if anyone knew jewels, Frances Blooming did. She owned four Cash for Golden Treasures stores. Tonight she was wearing enough gold on her petite five foot three inch tall body to warrant a police escort.

A woman on a mission, she paced around the casket, scrutinizing the necklace and earrings that adorned her friend. Pulling out her loupe, she bent down and peered at the jewels, turning them over and examining every inch of them.

Frances Blooming dug her hands into the deep folds of the blanket and grasped Ella Sandstrom's neck and ear. Next, she reached into her Louis

Vuitton gold-trimmed purse, pulled out a gold testing kit and set up shop, laying the kit on top of her friend's chest like a table. When she pulled out the acid, I stepped in.

"Ms. Blooming, I must interrupt. Forever-After liquid makeup isn't truly forever, and that acid could pose a problem for Mrs. Sandstrom's beauty sleep. We can remove the jewelry from Mrs. Sandstrom and then you may conclude your tests."

Frances Blooming looked up. Her eyes widened as she realized her former best friend was not a lab table, especially at her own funeral. We both gently picked up her kit and put the test vials back into the box.

"I'm sure it's a simple mix-up," I said to the distraught Mr. Sandstrom, whose arms now hung limply at his sides. He must have been in shock. His face didn't indicate any sign that he heard me. "I'm Melody Shore, funeral...assistant. If you would like to come with me, we can talk in private. I'm sure we can clear up this misunderstanding."

It was musical chairs in my office until I gave my desk chair to Ms. Blooming so she could sit next to David Sandstrom while I stood.

David Sandstrom's eyes filled with tears.

"I'm sure this is a misunderstanding. Explain to me what's wrong and I'm sure we can correct the problem immediately."

"I tried to honor her last request." He wiped his eyes and wrung his hands. "Her last request was to wear her favorite jewelry. What have you done with it? What kind of place is this? Why would you take a poor woman's jewelry from her deathbed?" He stood and rooted through the files on my desk, mixing my organized stacks together like a deck of playing cards. Maybe he thought the jewelry might be in the pile, or at least a receipt for me selling them on the black market?

"David," Frances Blooming said, her eyes laser-focused on my ill-fitting dress. "This young lady apparently doesn't know what she's doing."

"Where is Snugg, that no-good bastard?" screamed David Sandstrom.

"He has taken this 'stepping out' business too far." Frances shook her head. "I thought Edna Blair was exaggerating when she said he asked her sister-in-law out at her husband's funeral. That man is too much. He cannot leave The Peaceful Rest in chaos like this."

"Hang on a minute. Please excuse me for one second." I raced down the steps to the basement. Maybe I could solve this quickly. I yanked on the closet where we kept the deceased's personal items. But then I remembered, Snugg didn't give me the door code. What was he thinking? I can't do this.

"I demand an answer now," David Sandstrom shouted when I returned empty-handed. "I demand reimbursement for the jewels, and I demand a full refund for this entire service." He swept all the papers off my desk and shook his balled-up fists; his face turned a shade matching Frances Blooming's blouse. "What a damned waste," he said through pursed lips.

"I'm so sorry, Mr. Sandstrom." I pulled a tablet out of my drawer and a pen from my desk accessory holder and wrote his name and the words "missing jewelry," underlining the word missing. When I looked up, Frances Blooming's head was going back and forth like she was attending a tennis match between me and David Sandstrom. Miraculously, as I knelt to organize the strewn-about papers, the first thing I grabbed was a list of personal items for his wife.

"Here's the list," I read aloud. "A dress, undergarments, socks, shoes, and jewelry: fourteen karat gold-encased diamond earrings and necklace." There were no pictures, though. "Mr. Snugg normally takes and attaches a picture of the jewelry to the file," I said desperately. "Do you remember having the photo taken?" Instead of a photo, I saw some scribbles in the margin. Turning the paper over, I read, "$500,000." The form didn't have any time or date written, nor did it have the initials of the person who took the inventory. Snugg had told me this was a required procedure. My temples started to pulse, and I began to cough. I reached for the phone. "This has to be a mistake. Let me call Mr. Snugg."

"Did anyone else have access to Mrs. Sandstrom's belongings?" Frances Blooming asked.

"Well normally, Mr. Snugg..."

"This place has insurance, doesn't it? You have until tomorrow." Sandstrom hobbled from the room, his cane held high. He marched down the hall and out the funeral home doors without stopping in the Rose Room or even looking in its direction.

"Wait, David!" cried Ms. Blooming. She turned to me. "Have Arthur call me. Here's my card." She handed me a gold business card and hurried away into the night, which now seemed especially dark, if not foggy.

I held the phone for a while in my shaking hand, just staring into space.

Actually, I stared out into the empty lobby. All the visitors left during the hubbub. When I finally dialed Snugg's cell, it went straight to voicemail. On the fourth call, I left a message:

"Mr. Snugg, I need you to call me. The Sandstroms...well, Mr. Sandstrom and Frances Blooming...they claim we lost jewelry. Someone wrote $500,000 next to the jewelry description but didn't include a photo. The jewels are missing and I'm hoping they are locked up downstairs, but you didn't...uh, I don't have a door code. I'll see you in the morning at nine sharp and give you the full report. In fact, I'll go home and type it up and email it to myself–just in case we need to have a lawyer here tomorrow."

On the bus ride home, I leaned my head against the cool glass window trying to make sense of it. David Sandstrom didn't act the way I would expect. Who doesn't stick around for the visitation of his wife? Why did Frances Blooming run out after him? Could they be working together to pull insurance fraud on the funeral home? Inflating the jewelry value amount? A funeral home would be an easy target. Frances is a jewelry expert, and there was something fishy about David Sandstrom. He immediately asked for money for the jewelry and a reimbursement for the service, as though he had thought the list through beforehand.

Second thing, why didn't Snugg call me back, and why did he have me work tonight? Could he have stolen the jewels or sold them? Was he broke? A thief? No, that couldn't be. I'd known him since I was born. He was practically my godfather, even if he sometimes gave off a Dracula vibe.

By the time I got back to the apartment I wasn't sure if Snugg had run off with the jewels or if I would be fired for the mix-up. Tomorrow, I would tell him what happened. As I trudged up the steps beside the garage, I made my decision. I would figure out what happened to Ella Sandstrom's jewelry. I needed to do this for myself and for Snugg. I was not about to let anyone bamboozle me again.

Friday morning, Arthur Snugg stood huffing over my shoulder as we plowed through the file cabinet and all the papers on my desk.

"Why can't I find anything on Ella Sandstrom?" I slammed my file cabinet drawer and then pulled it open again and carefully shuffled through the files, hoping something would appear.

"He is claiming what, $500,000 worth of jewelry?" Snugg muttered for the fifth time. "It's got to be a typo. Tell me this is wrong, Melody." He smashed papers down on my desk. "Why didn't we fill out all the forms?"

"So the boys and you prepared Ella Sandstrom for viewing? How could her jewelry be wrong then?" I asked.

"It's the curse of my ex-wife Regina. She always took care of this and she said I couldn't handle it without her," Snugg said bitterly.

"I can't find anything. Let's call the boys!"

Snugg dialed and it immediately went to voicemail.

"Voicemail is lame. Text us and we'll get back to you if we aren't chugging our way to victory." The voice of the twins shouting in unison was almost deafening.

"What about J.J.? Doesn't he have a phone?" I wondered aloud.

"He lost it months ago. They share," Snugg sighed. "Stay here!" He stomped away to the lower-level storage room where I knew I didn't put any files, but I followed him and stood at the top of the stairs. Snugg bellowed an assortment of words too explicit to repeat. I could hear him taking out his frustrations on the boxes.

I looked through every email and phone record from the Sandstrom family and estate, but any mention of jewelry was missing. Snugg returned and paced back and forth in front of my office. He was like a circling shark.

"I've been thinking…" I stammered.

"In all our years, The Peaceful Rest has never lost anyone's possessions until you came onboard. Not my father, not my grandfather, not me. You hear me, Melody?"

"Until I came onboard?"

"Yes."

"You think I…I don't even have the code to the closet." I sighed. "Can I tell you my thoughts?"

"Your thoughts, your thoughts. I have a headache."

The phone rang. I pointed to the display:

"DAVID SANDSTROM."

"Tell him to hold. I'll take it upstairs."

I ate three stale mints from the spare bag in the desk drawer and stared at the blinking phone extension. What were they talking about? I wanted to know but I refused to eavesdrop. After a few deep mindful breaths, my heart rate slowed.

But I couldn't sit still, so I ran downstairs to the file room. A large antique desk stationed in the center of the tiny room was framed by a dozen dark filing cabinets. Someone stacked the cabinets on top of each other so high that they blocked any light that might've filtered through the glass block windows.

I found a stack of pristine, white, monogrammed notepads left by Regina Snugg. I preferred to write in cursive on white or yellow legal pads to think, but this would do. I jotted down my thoughts as they ticked in my mind like a cheap battery-powered wall clock:

Q1: Why would someone lay his wife out in $500,000 worth of jewelry?

  Why not keep the jewelry and sell it for more than the insurance money?

Q2: Who gets buried with earrings and necklace worth half a mil?

Q3: Why didn't he just sell the jewelry to Frances Blooming?

Q4: Frances Blooming? Relationship?

Q5: Where are Ella Sandstrom's jewels?

Q6: Did someone steal the jewelry? If so, who and why?

Once the police and reporters received word, everyone in the jewelry world would know. So this couldn't be theft, because any thief would know that resale would become virtually impossible. If stolen jewels did not sound plausible, what was the truth about the missing jewelry?

An idea came to me. Thankfully, I had been reorganizing the files by name instead of by year. A few drawers a day for three weeks already. Thank you, paralegal training. I yanked open a drawer that now housed last names beginning with S, and I searched every file.

Fifteen files in, I found something. Stuck in the back of Lois Schalmer's file, whose burial happened Tuesday, was a photo. Holding it up to the dim light coming through the windows, I saw a picture of jewelry.

The jewelry in the picture was a set of matching diamond earrings and a necklace– enormous diamonds with many prism cuts and gold encasement. The note on the back read, "Value, $500,000." It was followed by the initials DS or AS, most likely for Arthur Snugg. But if this was the correct set, where was it?

I was about to race upstairs to show Snugg when I heard the front door slam. Was David Sandstrom back? I counted to ten and continued on tiptoe, listening for any sort of arguing. It was silent. I was ten steps up the staircase to Arthur Snugg's office when I saw through his open door that his light was off. Back at my desk, Arthur Snugg had left a red ink scribbled note:

Meeting David Sandstrom to straighten this out. We need correct jewelry on his wife before tonight.

I peered into the two viewing rooms and out the window to the parking lot. All were empty. Well, except for Mrs. Sandstrom. I called Snugg's cell phone. It went again to voicemail. I didn't leave a message.

The two crystal floor lamps in the Rose Room were off. After a day of missing jewels, and the viewing being so poorly attended, Ella Sandstrom no longer looked peaceful. She looked more dead than yesterday if you know what I mean.

"Lord, help me. I need to find a clue," I whispered as I walked around the room a few times and then back to the casket.

Gritting my teeth, I bent over the body to examine the jewelry, ignoring the skin on her very powdered neck.

"Wait! Am I losing it? A different necklace than yesterday! This lady's jewelry changes more than Snugg changes women. First, the expensive necklace, now this necklace. I can't catch a break!" Someone was playing dress-up with Ella Sandstrom. I had no other choice. I counted to three, reached behind her neck, and removed the jewels. I needed someone who knew jewelry, and fast.

"Frances Blooming residence," a male voice answered.

"May I speak to Ms. Blooming? This is The Peaceful Rest Funeral Home. She requested the call."

"One moment."

I paced for a few minutes, spinning the butterfly beads on my bracelet wristwatch in rapid succession. As I was about to disconnect, someone picked up.

"Mr. Snugg, this is Frances Blooming."

"Ms. Blooming, this is Melody Shore."

"My word, you mean he can't even phone me back himself?"

"I'm sorry, he's on the other line. I will have him call you as soon as he can. I wouldn't have bothered you except there is something odd going on here with Mrs. Sandstrom's jewelry and you were the first person I could think of to ask."

"My expertise. Of course. I'll be right there."

"In this case, Ms. Blooming, I think I need to show you what I found. Why don't I bring them to your house?"

Frances Blooming's house sat atop a hill in the neighboring township of Foxmoor. Filled with large old foursquare homes and a three-block mom and pop business district, I'd been there often as a teenager to shop for clothes with Claire and her mom.

When I reached the address, I was speechless, and not from the cardio I got walking up her steep driveway. The house seemed bigger and creepier than I'd imagined–straight out of the "Addams Family." A crumbling brick tower jutted from the front of the house while cracked and missing tiles from its turret lay in the yard. Ancient soot from large, uncapped chimneys streaked the dilapidated roof.

I rang the bell on a rusted intercom box that hung off what used to be an ornate wrought-iron fence.

"May I help you?" the same deep male voice asked through the intercom speaker.

"Melody Shore to see Ms. Blooming."

Behind the overgrown bushes to my right, I made out a security camera eye. I turned and flashed a smile.

Click. The unmistakable sound of a camera.

"Please come in," the male voice cracked through the intercom and the gate jarred open.

A single flower trellis showing much love and care grew amongst an overgrown yard; the pruned roses climbed beautifully wild and covered every inch.

The inside of the house was in as much disarray as the outside. Frances Blooming greeted me in yoga pants and a T-shirt straight out of the movie Flashdance.

"Are those shoes Stuart Weitzman?"

"No. Someday, maybe." I reached down and brushed the driveway dust off my toe straps.

"Slip them off and follow," Frances said after pausing and thoughtfully staring at my shoes for too long.

She escorted me into a large room filled with exercise equipment. In the center of the room sat a concert hall size TV. An instructor stretched on the screen, giving motivational commands.

"I am right in the middle of my set, dear. Join me."

I picked up a mat and folded myself into the first pose.

"I've never done hot yoga before." I fake fanned myself.

Frances Blooming didn't reply.

After half twists, downward dog, modified cobra and some other poses I had never heard of, the tape finally ended. I fell onto my mat and wished I had worn more deodorant this morning. My beginning yoga class at Community College was not a prerequisite for this workout.

Every muscle in my body ached. Frances effortlessly jumped up off her mat, turned off the TV and walked to a nearby wingback sofa with peacock fabric pillows. She patted the seat next to her.

"Tell me, darling."

"I brought them in my purse."

I was about to hand her the jewelry when a man suddenly appeared in the doorway. He was broad-shouldered, tall, and had a head full of soft curly brown hair. I stared up at the gorgeous guy. What was a muscular, thirty-ish man with heavy-lidded Irish-whiskey brown eyes, and a day-old beard, doing as Frances Blooming's butler?

"Ms. Blooming, may I get you and your guest a lime spritzer or tonic?" he asked.

"I'm available—I mean…water please, if it's available. That would be great. Thank you."

"Water would be wonderful. Thank you, Russell." Frances waved him away.

Frances Blooming smiled at me. A big change from yesterday's encounter. I was about to pull out the costume jewelry when the water arrived. A rush of heat rose from my neck to my face, and it wasn't from the room temperature. I gulped the tonic water and the bitter taste sent me into a coughing attack. "Thanks," I said, my voice a mere squeak as he left again with a wink.

"Ms. Blooming." I tried to ask my questions. "I am here to…"

"Please call me Frances, Melody. Yoga friends don't call each other Ms."

I wanted to laugh, but Frances' eyes welled with tears. "Ella was a dear friend," she said, "and she didn't deserve this." Frances pulled out a photo from a folder on the coffee table. I could only guess it was the missing jewelry.

"Wow, those are beautiful." I held the photo up to the light. It matched mine.

"I remember when Ella bought these." Frances pointed to the photo. "We were together at an auction. She said David's investments were really paying off, and she wanted to give herself an anniversary gift. The necklace and earrings are eighteen karat gold with round briolette diamonds."

"Thank you, Frances. That confirms that the photo I have is correct and we are both looking for the right necklace."

"Both looking? You don't suspect me then?" Frances said with eyebrows raised.

"No. I can tell you cared about her very much, and…you…Now, I don't want this to shock you, but today when I went to visit Mrs. Sandstrom, her jewelry was not the same as it was yesterday. Yesterday she wore diamonds. Similar to the picture of the missing ones, with the same large diamond in the center and shining like anything. We both saw them. But not the same as the beautifully cut large ones in the photo. Yesterday's were maybe cubic zirconia? Today, she was wearing these. I brought them as they are completely wrong." I reached into my purse and carefully pulled out the plastic grocery bag containing the jewelry I removed from Ella Sandstrom's neck an hour earlier. Teardrop shaped glass beads. Blue tinted!

"Look at this."

Frances studied the laughably fake beads just for a moment then she picked up the picture of the missing real jewelry.

"Aside from the drop shape cut of the stones, that is where the similarity ended. See the smoothness of the crystals? Real briolette diamonds have many facets. The jewelry last evening and the ones you brought today are costume jewelry."

"Who do you think would have a motive? Who would do this?" I stood up and walked over to roll up the yoga mats.

"You don't think someone stole the jewelry, do you?" Frances said.

"No. I mean…I don't know what to think. It doesn't make any sense. Did she have any enemies?"

"Why would you say that?" Frances asked.

"I don't know, but I'm trying to find them. The diamonds. My job depends on this."

"Your job? I'd say Snugg's job is more on the line. Someone there is messing around with the Sandstroms and throwing blame on The Peaceful Rest." Frances walked over, took the yoga mats from my hands, and returned to her sofa. "What about Snugg? Could he have something to do with the missing jewels?" Frances motioned for me to sit down again. "I heard he brought Roseanna Moore white lilies on a date out of season. Who knows, he might get a hankering to give someone expensive jewelry."

"But who would steal from themselves and believe they wouldn't get caught?" I cried.

"It does seem unlikely, but where was he?"

"I'll find out. He does date a lot." I laughed. "Snugg is rough around the edges, and I don't know where he was last night, but he doesn't deserve an accusation that he stole half a million dollars."

"Does he seem shocked they are missing?" Frances asked.

"He's really upset. Mr. Snugg put his trust in me, and I want to help Mr. Sandstrom. It's hard enough to lose someone without this." I gently removed the fake blue beads from her hand.

"That's pretty admirable. What a dear you are. Imagine caring for that ridiculous David Sandstrom. The way he treated Ella was a dreadful shame. Don't fall for his crocodile tears." Frances took a sip of her water and set it down like a gavel. "I can keep my eyes open and inquire with my contacts in the jewelry world to see if he has pulled any nonsense."

"Oh, thank you."

"But Melody, if someone has stolen the jewels, what can you possibly do? You are in no position to find them any more than Snugg can."

"Until last month, I had been running the admin for a large law firm in Pitt. Let me tell you, Frances, that my admin skills are impeccable. I will find out who stole this jewelry if the only clue I have is a trail of spent staples."

Frances Blooming laughed a loud peal of laughter and clapped her hands. "They better watch out then, shouldn't they, Melody? Oh, I haven't laughed like this in some time. Why don't you let me help? If someone tries to sell them, I will know." She handed me another business card.

"Ms. Blooming, I mean Frances, do you believe that note we found— that $500,000 is an accurate value for the jewelry she was supposed to wear?"

"Sentimental value, yes. Actual value, more like $300,000."

"Why would anyone lay someone out in such expensive jewels?" I asked.

"Grief can make people do crazy things," Frances said.

"It sure does." A tremor went up my spine. "When my dad passed away, my mom immediately sold his collection of baseball jerseys. I didn't get a single one."

"Oh my, that is sad."

"Frances, would you be willing to verify the jewelry value with Snugg and give us more information about the local market?"

"I can do that. And I won't even charge him a valuation fee. I want to help too." Frances looked at me thoughtfully. "You remind me a lot of my daughter, Liz."

"Does she live nearby?"

"Sadly, she passed several years ago in a car crash…from a drunk driver," Frances said, her voice breaking.

"I'm sorry to hear that."

"I've let the place go a little since then. You know she was about to marry when she died. It hurt really bad–I'll tell you. Real bad. Now, I've got no grandkids, no one to pass things on to." Frances waved her hand frivolously in the air as though the crumbling mansion were worth a great deal. I searched for something helpful to say.

"Well, my dad used to say when you love someone, they live on in your heart, and that's why I have to find these jewels. Mr. Snugg, he gave me a job when I had nowhere else to turn. I have to help him find the jewelry. I can't let him down now."

"Aw, dear, you are a wonder. I've just put it together. Shore. Your dad was Snugg's partner back in the day, wasn't he? He sounds like he was a kind and intuitive man," Frances said, patting my hand. "Be grateful while you have him."

"But he died when I was sixteen." I wipe a tear which had formed on my eye and was threatening to spill onto my cheek.

"No. I mean, yes, hon. What I mean is Mr. Snugg. The old Dracula needs a good friend right now, and you are practically family. I'm glad he has you to help him."

"What will we do? We don't have any leads."

"You know, I think you can find the jewelry, Melody!" Frances stood up.

"I can?"

"Yes. You are a smart girl. You have skills. Not yoga skills, but…"

I couldn't help laughing embarrassingly loud at that one, but Frances kept going without batting an eyelash.

"How you remind me of my daughter. She was a legal secretary too. And we know what that means."

"Yes, I do, Frances. It means we know how to spot a mistake. I have the best administration skills on this planet. I can spot a comma splice from 10,000 feet. Somewhere, that thief made a mistake bigger than filling the bond paper tray with plain white paper or putting caffeinated coffee in the decaf dispenser!"

"You are so right! The thief has left a clue, and you, my dear Melody, are just the person to find it. I know it. Everything will work out. Believe you me." Frances picked up a box of tissues from the nearby end table and offered it to me.

I blew my nose.

Frances glanced up at the wall clock, which read twelve thirty-five p.m. and grasped my hand.

"I've got to go downtown in an hour. Please, come back tomorrow at the same time and we will do yoga and work on this mystery some more. Ta-ta!" She hurried out of the room.

I checked my phone. No messages. I needed to get back and tell Arthur

Snugg what I'd learned. I wrote my name and number on the back of Frances' business card and laid it on top of the tissue box. She might need it in case she thinks of any other details. Also, there was no harm leaving my number around for that good-looking Russell to find.

Once again, as if the air whispered his name, Russell appeared in the doorway.

"Would you like a ride back? I noticed you didn't come in a car."

"You can leave during working hours?"

"Yes, I'm headed out myself."

"Thank you. A ride to the funeral home would be nice."

Out in the yard, I nodded to the flower trellis. "Is gardening your talent, Mr. Russell?"

"Growing flowers is like romance. Time and patience are both required," he said, opening the door to the passenger side of his Ford F-150, blue of course.

I hid my face with a fake cough and jumped into the seat. When we pulled out onto the roadway, classic rock burst through the speakers. He reached for the knob to turn it off, but hesitated.

"This okay, Melody?"

"Depends who I am listening to it with," I yelled over the music. "Do you like yoga, Russell?"

"Depends who I am doing it with, Melody." He turned his head toward me and smiled, revealing two adorable dimples I hadn't noticed earlier.

"Can I ask how you became Ms. Blooming's assistant?" I shouted a little too loudly as Russell turned the sound down so we could talk.

"What makes you think I'm her assistant?" he said.

He's right. I was suddenly flummoxed. He could be her boyfriend, or some kind of bodyguard. I wasn't sure. I smoothed my hair behind my ears and brushed some dust off my clothes from the hot yoga.

"Well, you answered the intercom, you offered us a drink. Those are the qualities of a personal assistant. Wait, are you teasing me? You are her assistant, right?"

"You have me figured out," Russell said as we turned onto Republic Street toward the funeral home.

"You didn't tell me your last name."

"Russell McCormick. I moved here a few years ago."

"Oh, where from?"

"Texas. A small town close to Austin. Have you ever been?"

"No, but I heard everything is bigger in Texas. I mean...never mind. No, I have never been anywhere south of West Virginia." A slow song started on the radio. We both sat quietly until I asked, "So, do you know David Sandstrom?"

"I know his wife and Frances Blooming were good friends. I've been there when they were over for dinner."

"Then you are her personal assistant?"

"So, your job is assistant at The Peaceful Rest?"

Avoiding a response. Interesting. I tried another approach. "Okay, but, what did you think...of them from your observations at Ms. Blooming's house? Did they seem to have a good relationship?"

Russell turned his head quizzically as a buzz and some garbled language emitted from the pocket of his jacket.

"Sorry," he said as we pulled into the parking lot. "I have to get back to work."

"It was great to meet you, Russell," I said. "You know where to find me if you need an experienced yoga partner."

Arthur Snugg sat in my office chair and stared at my computer screen. The file cabinet drawers were open, and papers were everywhere.

"Mr. Snugg, I'm sorry. I forgot to sign off before I left. It won't happen again." I started to shut the file cabinets.

"Melody, I have to come right out and ask you something." His usual father-like voice was replaced by a strained grumble as he stared angrily at my browsing history. "Did you take the jewelry?"

"Oh, Mr. Snugg, no. No, I didn't take the jewelry. I found the picture of the missing jewelry and when I came upstairs to show you, you were gone. So, I went out to see Frances Blooming...and..."

"What? Melody, show me the picture you found." He thrust his hand, palm up, at me like an unhappy landlord trying to collect his overdue rent.

I pulled the picture out of my purse and Arthur Snugg looked at it for a long minute. "I have never seen this picture...Wait. Melody! Frances

Blooming?" His voice boomed through the entire funeral home.

"I don't want the funeral home charged with anything, even an insurance claim, so I went to Frances to..."

"Or no, wait...no...do you think she stole the jewelry?" he said loudly.

"No. She offered to help us find the jewels for free." I walked back and forth in the six foot of space in my office like a goldfish swimming in circles. I knew neither one of us could be working with Frances, and she seemed completely reliable. However, the more I thought about it, maybe Frances Blooming's business wasn't doing well. Her house looked run down as if she didn't have the resources to repair it, but I was pretty sure Frances was not the thief. She seemed extremely unhappy that the theft hurt her friend's last wishes. While she could do a lot of repairs with the money from the missing jewelry, she didn't seem to be the type. Finally, I gave up. "I did yoga with her," I said, "and no one who does that much yoga can be a thief."

He scowled at me with a loud humph. He held out his hand to shush me, his eyes on my computer monitor: "Police question business owner regarding investment fraud." Below it, a picture of Frances Blooming.

"Melody, don't tell me you think I am working with Frances Blooming to steal the jewelry? That's not why you went to talk to her, is it?"

"It's good investigating to ask everyone. You didn't take them, did you?" I asked him.

"No! I didn't take the jewelry, nor am I in cahoots with Frances as a smuggler." Snugg crossed his arms and shook his head. "What did Frances Blooming say?" He pulled on his formerly smooth hair, raking it until it stuck out like horns.

"Ms. Blooming says David Sandstrom inflated the jewelry value of the necklace and accessories. They are not worth half a million, even with combined value. They are more like 300K. Frances said she'd come out and value it, for free." I sat down in my guest chair as Snugg was still occupying my desk seat.

"How does that help? If we had the jewelry, we wouldn't need it valued. For goodness' sake, Melody, I have had enough of this kerfuffle." Arthur Snugg covered his eyes. I stared at the photo, then pressed it against my head to rack my brain for any more clues.

"What about David Sandstrom?" I asked. "What did he say earlier today?"

"Yes, he has agreed to let us continue with his wife's second viewing tonight. Of course, the burial tomorrow, Saturday, is still as scheduled."

"Well, that's a good sign, I guess."

"I will need your help again tonight, if you can make it."

"Wait. You didn't say before, but I need to know." I stood up and got a clean legal pad and a fresh pen. "Mr. Snugg, where were you last night? Why didn't you answer your phone or call back?"

"Well, it's only fair." Snugg stood up and buttoned his suit and smoothed his tie. "I was on a date, if you must know, with Helen Blair. She took over as manager at Jim's Jeeps when her husband passed away."

"Yes, but what does that have to do with you not answering your phone?"

"Well, to be honest, I was distracted. We took a lot of self-thingies and I forgot to charge my phone. We were in her jeep for a long time." Snugg sighed. "Which reminds me, Melody. Next time there is an emergency—"

"Yes, Mr. Snugg?"

"Just text me what the emergency is."

"Text you? How would that help if you had a dead phone battery?" I threw my notepad down and jammed the pen back in its holder. "And it's called a selfie."

Before I could say anything else, his phone rang. He muttered a few explicit words under his breath and stepped out of my office. I couldn't make out everything he said, but I did hear the words, "I won't pay you a cent."

He stepped back. "This week has been awful. I've been trying to pass on to you and the boys some of Regina's former duties, but now those jewels are missing and Regina's lawyer is all over me."

"That's awful, Mr. Snugg. I can see why you are upset."

Snugg walked downstairs and he must have gone to the floral room. He returned to the foyer with a small peace lily. He fluffed it and arranged it on an end table. Then, he picked up a "Handling Grief and Tough Times" brochure and turned his back to me, silently reading. After a moment, he loudly blew his nose.

"Listen, Mr. Snugg, you hired me when I needed a job, I will give you that…but then you turn around and put me solely in charge of the viewing. You didn't even leave me the door code and you accused me of theft?

Do you want my help tonight? Then I want overtime. And when I find the jewels…I want a raise."

Arthur Snugg stood quietly for a moment. I was about to walk out when he said, "Deal." Snugg extended his hand to shake. "Melody, I should have given you the belongings' closet code when you started. The code is the same as the floral room and any other lock in the funeral home."

"Three-one-eight?"

"Yeah, my ex-wife's birthday. I'm sorry for not trusting you sooner," Arthur Snugg said. Suddenly we were a team again.

"Thank you, Mr. Snugg. Now I, Melody Shore, am on the missing accessories case," I said with a grin. "I'm sure someone will say something about the jewelry at the viewing. I will stay in the room and mingle."

"Hmm." Snugg walked over to the large painting of his father hanging in the foyer and straightened the frame. "Tonight's visitors—probably half of the township's high society—will come to pay their respects. We will both keep our eyes and ears open."

An hour before the viewing, I remembered that the second set of jewelry that I took to show Frances Blooming was still in my purse. Arthur Snugg's phone extension was blinking red. He was probably on the phone with his lawyer. After several deep breaths and two walks to the casket, I turned around and ran back out of the Rose Room. I had laid the second set of incorrect jewelry back on Ella Sandstrom. It wasn't clasped but it would have to do.

I was halfway through a fresh box of tissues in the ladies' guest room, dabbing my eyes and blowing my nose, when the door swung open and Claire Cottage walked in.

"Why are you here in the guest bathroom? I've looked all over for you."

"Because the staff bathroom is just for men. I'm thinking we should reverse this soon." I pulled out my compact, saw my puffy face, and snapped it back shut.

"Melody, you look terrible. That's a real Betsy Johnson purse, I would know, and you're so red from crying that it looks blue."

"The mirror is vintage, but the makeup is refilled by a specialty company," I said, sniffing and squinting to keep from crying. "I mail it to this place in New York to get a refill." I looked at Claire and pinched my nose to try and keep the emotions in, but it wasn't working. One look at my reflection in the mirror and I started to bawl.

"Melody, please don't cry." Her voice carried through the bathroom and probably out into the foyer. "This place freaks me out. What is going on, Melody? I heard all over town that there was a robbery here last night and some people think you did it. Some people say Snugg. The vote seems to oscillate between the two of you."

"Me?" My tears start to flow again. "I ran around all day trying to find out what happened to the jewels. Then I come back and Snugg accuses me. Now you are telling me that others are too? This is hopeless."

"Calm down, Melody. You wouldn't steal candy from a baby. Everyone knows about the time our algebra teacher, 'Flunk-You-for-No-Reason-Fulmer,' accidentally left the final test answers at your house when he dated your mom and you gave them back without looking at them and skirted through the class with a C minus. They will all remember how honest you are when the missing jewelry shows up. Now listen, I brought you something to cheer you up." She handed me a dress carrier bag.

"Aw, thank you!" I unzipped the bag and found a royal blue A-line dress and a silver jacket. My eyes welled with tears again. "You are so amazing, Claire."

Claire wrapped her arms around me and we hugged.

"Claire, I need to ask you something. Do you know Frances Blooming?" I said as I darted behind the Japanese screen to change out of my sweaty yoga clothes from earlier.

"Well, nothing good about her," Claire grunted as she pushed a heavy wingback chair closer so she could sit down. "I say 'nothing good' with some authority because we are in fact neighbors."

"What do you know about her? Oh, and did you bring any stockings?"

Around the screen, Claire handed me her phone and a plastic egg filled with rather high-quality gray stockings.

The phone is open to a photo of Claire's vintage dress shop decorated with flags. Two doors down is a strange stone and gold gilded building. A neon sign read, "CASH for Golden Treasures" and the trim was painted gold.

"Her store has been nothing but trouble since it opened," Claire said.

"What do you mean? She seemed so nice when I visited her today."

"Cash for gold and those pawn shops and check-cashing stores, they weaken our local economy and erode our community's character. She says she's a gold buyer, but that's not what I think. I have seen police there and some shady people go in and out."

"Really? That's interesting. And one more question…" I gestured for help with the zipper.

"No, Melody, now me. What happened last night?"

"The jewels Mr. Sandstrom said were on his wife aren't there. They are very pricey and for some reason no one here seems to remember them being checked in. Even the forms were absent and the files mixed up. There're insurance issues no matter how we look at it."

I left my bag behind the screen. I was going to need a locker or cabinet in here. "Have you ever seen this guy?" I showed a picture of David Sandstrom and his wife from the obit on my phone.

"Maybe you should call the police, Melody. Missing jewelry. Money. Gold. It sounds dangerous."

"No. I'm looking for jewelry that was supposed to be on a dead body. I don't think it's dangerous. The only dangerous thing at this point is losing my job." I gave the stockings one last waist tug.

"Oh, Melody, you can work at my shop, you know it. You could even live with me if you needed to."

"I appreciate that, Claire." I spun around a few times, admiring myself in the mirror. "But at this rate, I will be someone's assistant until I die. Well, I guess I'm in the right place for that. You know what I mean." I laughed. Claire pealed her fluttery laughter.

"I get you, girl. You want to be the woman in charge. So you go out there and get it."

We grabbed some coffee in the kitchenette and Claire said her goodnight. Then I was left with a simple task: Find a half-million-dollar set of jewels and make sure Snugg and The Peaceful Rest weren't blamed for their loss. Well, at least I looked good enough to blend in. I was sure I could dig up some more info from the family. Maybe they wouldn't even recognize me from last night. I mean, it's not like I stood out or anything.

I wandered into the Rose Room just in time for the crowd. It's amazing what a simple dress and jacket do for first impressions. After the initial looks, the viewers continued their deep, private conversations. No one took a second look.

"Poor David. On top of losing his beloved wife, I heard they lost her jewelry too," said a lady with a teal infinity scarf looped a little too tightly around her neck.

"I heard Frances Blooming wants David to sue the funeral home and Arthur Snugg for all his pain and suffering," whispered an owlish-looking gentleman to a tall, carrot-red haired woman.

"David wouldn't do that. He and Ella are such good people," she answered as she removed his glasses from his face and cleaned them with a tissue.

Hunched in a chair next to the casket was David Sandstrom.

I walked to the casket and paid my respects to Ella Sandstrom for the first time.

"Hi, Ella," I whispered. I bowed my head and pretended to pray but opened my eyes the tiniest bit to make a mental impression of tonight's jewels. They were the same ones I removed earlier and then bravely placed back on her. Sandstrom hasn't said anything. Maybe my luck was changing. But my reprieve was short-lived. When I stood and turned away from the casket, the heel of my shoe cracked and broke halfway off.

I looked around, hoping nobody had noticed. Above the crowd, I caught sight of a familiar pair of broad shoulders with a head of curly brown hair. Russell! What was he doing here? Did he bring Frances Blooming? I scanned the room but didn't see her. I forgot to ask if she'd be here tonight.

Although I wanted to get to know Russell on a much deeper level, now was not the time. I turned my back to him and exited the room, heel dragging.

At the top of the stairs, I slipped off my shoes and tiptoed down to the floral room. It was the only room besides the file room in the lower level I wanted to access.

My fingers hurriedly punched in the code, three-one-eight, and the glass door opened.

The smell of flowers in the room mixed with my recent sighting of Russell, and I was momentarily intoxicated. I felt like a buzzing bee in a field of pollen-filled flowers. As I stood there, it hit me. Grant, my doofus ex who talked with his mouth full, would have never proposed to me. I mean, he had never given me flowers, not once—and I expected a ring! Actually, now that I thought about it, not a single man in my twenty-eight years of life had ever given me flowers. I was sure if a guy ever did, he wouldn't know what hit him. I would have dumped roses on the floor and rolled around in them right then. That's what one second with Russell did to me. He was like a loaded beefy burrito and a buy-one-get-one margarita. Well, better than that.

Focus, focus.

I threw my useless shoes down, and collapsed to the floor against the glass door, trying to figure out my next move. A large hole and snag had formed in the right foot of the stocking. I pulled off the stockings and threw them onto the floral room prep table. Why did I have to make things "perfect" all the time? My stupid vintage heels let me down. Why couldn't I just be normal like everyone else and wear sensible shoes? Was I a colossal idiot for trying to solve this crime as though I were some private detective? I had no clues. I had no necklace. Instead, I was barefoot and drooling over flowers in the basement where I was supposed to be working – where I was supposed to be professional, be calm, and find a hideous set of jewelry that cost half a million dollars so I could keep my hideous job!

As I stood up, I heard a man and a woman coming down the stairs. It was Frances Blooming and David Sandstrom, and it sounded like they were arguing. Why were they coming downstairs? There were restrooms upstairs.

Besides the vases of roses, lilies, and gladiolas, there was a large prep table, a glass cooler with shelves, and a few dozen flattened flower boxes on a shelf. The only other thing in the room was a barely-used chest freezer with a thermostat that didn't work. Everyone complained it was more like a refrigerator than a freezer. I opened the lid and peeked in. Nothing in it—plenty of room for me. I climbed in the freezer. My pinky finger held the lid open an unnoticeable amount.

"If I wanted your advice, Frances, I would have asked you. But I didn't!" David Sandstrom grumbled loudly.

"This whole thing needs to end, David. I spoke to Melody. Snugg doesn't have Ella's jewelry and he doesn't have the money to pay you their value."

"They got you fooled. No wonder you and my wife were friends."

"Don't make me alert the authorities, David. Ella told me she suspected you were doing something illegal. What is it? What have you done? And now this! Are you pulling a scam to get money out of The Peaceful Rest instead of honoring my best friend on her deathbed?"

"I want those jewels back! You better stay out of my way, if you know what's good for you." David Sandstrom slammed his hand on the floral room glass door.

Frances Blooming stormed out of the lower level "Emergency Exit" and David Sandstrom hobbled back upstairs, breathing heavily. I pushed open the freezer, and jumped out. My arms and legs were bright red. Broken thermostat or not, the freezer wasn't a pleasant temperature.

At the top of the staircase stood Arthur Snugg.

"Melody, where are your shoes? Why are your arms and legs covered with goose bumps? Are you sick?"

"It's a long story."

"Most people are on their way out. We should be done here soon. Let me give you a ride home. It's pouring outside." Snugg set a pair of monogrammed "R.S." rain boots on my desk. "I'm exhausted. I'm sure you are too."

"Yes, I am," I answered as I looked down at my feet.

"I've been thinking. We have nothing to prove we aren't at fault here. Let's end this. I might as well file an insurance claim." He inhaled deeply. "My rates are high already...this won't be good, but I don't see another option. Let's fill it out tonight and get Sandstrom's signature if we can before he leaves right now. I'd hate for there to be tension at the burial too. I'll go upstairs and email the form to you."

He didn't wait for an answer. As he headed up the mahogany staircase to his office, another group of mourners quietly filed by and out the funeral home doors.

Within fifteen minutes, I'd completed the form Snugg emailed me.

"Mr. Snugg, you need to sign this before I make a copy," I called up to his office. No reply. The upstairs was eerily quiet, so I wandered back to the Rose Room in search of Snugg.

In the viewing room, the lights were off except for a beam of light from a flashlight. A man was bent over the casket. I could make out that it was David Sandstrom. Everyone had left him. Odd, but I decided to give him a few moments. I walked quietly toward my office, but a tickle started in my nose and I sneezed.

David Sandstrom emerged from the Rose Room, the gun in his hand pointed straight at me.

"What are you doing? Mr. Sandstrom, a gun isn't the answer." I waved the paper in my hand. "Mr. Snugg has already filled out your insurance claim. I have it right here."

"Insurance money…that would be icing on the cake, but I don't really need it. I have loads of cash, but it's the jewels I want back."

"We don't have them. We are trying to find them."

"Your time has run out!"

"Why do you think we took your wife's jewels?"

"You must have," he said through gritted teeth.

"Did you really ever bring them here in the first place?" I asked.

"Quit asking questions. Stupid nosy people like you and your incompetent boss. Where are my wife's jewels?" He pointed the gun at my chest.

"Are you looking for diamonds? I don't have them, MR. SANDSTROM." I shouted his name, as if help would magically appear, but the only other soul was his dead wife in the Rose Room, and she wasn't moving.

"Don't play dumb with me," he said with both hands on his gun.

"Why did you lay your wife out in such expensive jewelry if you didn't want the insurance money? You know we didn't take them, so why this whole charade?"

"I was trying to do one thing right in our marriage: honor her wishes, lay her out in them. But of course, I wanted to take them back before her burial. She doesn't need the jewelry now. Someone else might as well enjoy them. And you beat me to it."

"That's a horrible thing to say. I didn't take your wife's jewelry. Why would I?" I inched a few more steps backward. I felt hands on my back, but I didn't dare turn around.

Suddenly, Frances Blooming stepped in front of me, partially blocking Sandstrom. "David, put the gun down," Frances commanded. "I came back when I was informed you were spouting craziness, and I see I was right. You've become unhinged."

"I'm going to take care of both of you here and now." David Sandstrom clicked the gun safety off.

"With your poor dead wife in the next room?" I gasped.

"You're right. I need time to get out of the country. Come on." He pointed his gun toward the lower-level staircase. "Show me around. I bet there are lots of places downstairs to hide bodies."

At the word bodies, Arthur Snugg jumped out from around the corner.

"Mr. Snugg!" I shouted.

"Oh great, I should have known you would still be here too. Well, now, I will just have to get rid of all three of you." Sandstrom gestured at us with his gun. "Bang, bang, and bang." He advanced as the three of us backed into my tiny office.

"Mr. Sandstrom, I assure you, we didn't steal or take the jewels. It was an accident. In fact, I know where the jewels must be. If you let these two go, I'll show you." I motioned to the Rose Room, hoping Snugg and Frances would play along with my bluff. Frances Blooming stood firm in her spot. Arthur Snugg said nothing but inched toward my doorway.

David Sandstrom ran forward and violently shoved Snugg. On the way down, Snugg's head connected with the corner of my file cabinet, and he collapsed in a heap. The cabinet rocked and my new nameplate fell off. David Sandstrom kicked him, but Arthur Snugg didn't flinch.

"Let me help him! His head is bleeding!" I cried, hovering over Mr. Snugg's unconscious body.

"Don't touch him. I'll finish him off after. Ladies first…in fact, I think we will make this look like a sad suicide from a poor unbalanced woman who stole my jewelry, killed her boss, and then the rich gold lady."

Down the steps he pushed Frances first, then me, the gun barrel pressed into my lower back.

"David, you've gone over the edge. Stop this nonsense. Put that gun away." Frances's voice was shaking.

"I told you, Frances, to stay out of my business."

"Your wife was my friend. Melody is my friend. You aren't making sense."

"Sense? My wife got too noisy. Like you two ladies. Wanted to know where I got my money. When she found out, she threatened to turn me in to the police. I stopped her and I'll stop you." He pointed the gun at Frances.

My eyes were open so wide they hurt. Did he just confess to murdering his wife?

David Sandstrom shoved me forward into Frances Blooming, and we were slowly backing towards the floral room.

"Open it," he screamed. I punched in the code and he pushed us into the room.

"My wife used my money that I stole from unsuspecting investors to purchase her expensive jewelry. My clients thought they were making money in 'Great Gains Investments.' Yeah, they were." He spouted an evil laugh. "On paper, they were making money, and I was taking their money."

"You're horrible! You think you can redeem yourself by putting jewelry bought with illegal money on your poor deceased wife, and that will make up for everything?"

"Shut up!"

By sheer luck, I stumbled into my broken heels and my Betsy Johnson clutch purse.

In one swift yoga move, Frances Blooming grabbed the heel of my broken shoe, whirled around, and slammed it into Sandstrom's eye.

Screaming, he grabbed his face with his right hand and stumbled backward. His gun went off, the bullet shearing an entire vase of gladiolas from their stems, which then toppled over and shattered.

Frances Blooming turned pale, gripped her heart, ripping her western style turquoise bead necklace, and collapsed onto the prep table. Necklace beads rolled everywhere.

"Frances!" I screamed. Rage boiled up through me. "Now you've done it." I turned angrily to Sandstrom who stood stunned, blood oozing down his face from the gash in his eye.

Then his neck muscles bulged, his face reddened, and he came at us. I had nothing on me except my purse. I reached in, found my vintage gold lipstick, and quickly rolled it on the floor. Sandstrom took two more steps, the last one square on the tube. Losing his balance, he slid backwards and fell onto his back.

Before he could move, I grabbed my other shoe and struck him with the other heel. I kept hitting him anywhere I could reach with everything I had. I hit him over and over with my shoe, my compact makeup mirror, and even my vintage lipstick case until I felt a hand on my shoulder.

It was Russell, accompanied by a police officer and a paramedic. The officer pulled David Sandstrom to his feet and cuffed him. I collapsed in Russell's arms, sobbing.

"We were running down here to save you, but you seem to have everything pretty well in the bag," Russell said.

We walked upstairs where two more police officers were waiting in my office. The paramedics had moved Arthur Snugg to the foyer and were tending to him. I grasped Snugg's hand and thankfully he returned the squeeze.

Frances Blooming was brought upstairs on the elevator on a stretcher, and the paramedics were hooking her up to IVs.

"I came to the funeral home earlier this evening," Russell said, still holding me. "But I didn't see you. Thankfully your boss called us and said there was a situation."

"We were across the street at the bar. We saw all the cop cars," shouted J.J., running in the door with Alex.

David Sandstrom, handcuffed, was taken away by the police. The paramedics took Frances Blooming out to a waiting ambulance. Snugg sat with a large ice pack taped to his head.

"Uncle Arthur, are you okay? Melody, what happened?" Alex cried.

"That man over there—Sandstrom—he just admitted to killing his wife. He tried to kill all three of us...Frances, she saved us," I said, my voice breaking. I squeezed my eyes shut and looked upward. "But I think she had a heart attack."

"Thanks to you, Melody, Sandstrom's not going to hurt anyone now," Russell said as he let me stand on my own again.

"He confessed to me that he stole from his clients," I added. "He stole the money they trusted him to invest. He doctored the reports, so it looked like they were making money, but they weren't."

"Dang! Man, Melody, you're like all detective and stuff," J.J. said.

"Yes, she is, and my officers are impressed at the injuries inflicted by a broken shoe and the contents of a purse. They are considering requisitioning them the next time weapon requests become available." Russell winked.

"Vintage never lets me down," I said as I closed my now-empty clutch purse with a snap. "Course, now the bow is ripped, but it held up well under pressure, proving its worth…" I stopped as Russell handed me back my gold lipstick tube, now dented, and it reflected off his sergeant's badge hanging on his belt buckle.

"Wow, Russell, you're a cop!"

Russell's brown eyes gazed steadily at me. How good could this guy get? He's a cop who likes flowers and yoga…and maybe, just maybe, a girl like me.

"I knew your biceps were too big for a yoga assistant," I said as he helped me into his patrol car to take us to the hospital.

On the following Wednesday, Arthur Snugg limped into my newly reorganized office and laid another file on my desk.

"Melody, I'm so sorry to hear Frances didn't survive her heart attack."

"I know, Mr. Snugg. I'm glad I went to the hospital to see her. Her heart attack caused too much damage. They tried to do surgery, but…" Arthur Snugg handed me a tissue. "I can't stop thinking about her kindness. We wouldn't be here if it weren't for her coming back to the funeral home and saving us. I just can't believe she's gone." I picked up the gold-colored yoga block I had purchased on my way to work and set it in a prominent place on my desk, next to my coffee warmer.

"If you're up to it, I would like you to help with tonight's viewing for her," Snugg said.

That evening, all the city's high society turned out to pay their last respects to Frances Blooming. High-priced cars and SUVs which brought the prominent population of Pleasantview and Foxmoor filled the parking lot. Alex and J.J. assisted as door attendants.

Dressed in my emerald green swing dress and my new matching Mary Jane heels, I entered the Lilac Room. Now that I had survived my first three weeks at The Peaceful Rest, I was certain vintage was in.

Frances was right…everything will work out.

The light purple walls and table lamp cast soft light on the woman who I had so recently met. I whispered to her, wishing we were back in her sitting room.

"I wish we could have spent more time together. You were truly golden to me."

After the prayer service, I saw Russell standing in the back of the room with a dozen roses and a clasp envelope in his hand.

"Frances Blooming's attorney came by the station today. Frances called him on Saturday after you left her hospital room. She refused to be taken into surgery until he'd changed her will. I was told by her attorney that you needed to see the change she made—and I needed to see you again. I hope bringing flowers isn't weird, I mean, uh—being you're around them all day…"

"Yeah, normally the florist brings them, but…that's sweet of you." I inhaled the scent of the flowers. I needed a moment to hide my grin, compose myself, and slow down my pounding heart.

"I was wondering if you wanted to go out sometime. Do something fun?"

"You mean our first two encounters weren't fun?"

He chuckled and I tore open the envelope.

Addendum

I, Frances Blooming, being of sound mind and a youthful body, do hereby leave my personal jewelry collection, my yoga tape collection and my "Stuart Weitzman" shoes to my new friend, Melody Shore, because with the right accessories anything is possible. The rest of my estate shall be divided between the various charities as I previously stated in my Will.

My personal jewelry collection is held under lock and key in a safety deposit box at the bank described in Exhibit A of my Last Will and Testament and has an approximate value of $48,000.

Alex and J.J. wandered over to my office after the mourners left.

"I'm glad you were still able to make Saturday's non-qualifier Beer Olympics, but I need the Harriet Carter file stat."

"I'm just glad we were still at the bar getting extra beer for our trip Friday night when Sandstrom attacked. Here, everything is in the file how you wanted." Alex handed me the guest book and file for Harriet Carter.

I spread the file's contents out on my desk. The list of deceased belongings read: dress, undergarments, socks and shoes, necklace and earrings. Then I saw the initials A.S. That was when I realized. A.S. wasn't Arthur Snugg, it was Alex Smith!

"Where was this?" I asked.

"Sorry, Mel. It was down in our office under the mail on our desk. We didn't see you on Friday when we came back to get the Beer Olympics flyer." Alex punched J.J. in the arm.

"It's not my fault." J.J. punched his brother back and then ducked behind me for cover. "We needed the flyer to get the free cooler."

"Why didn't you return my and your uncle's calls?"

"We shut our phone off. You know, to focus on the Olympics," J.J. said. "It helped too, we got second in beer pong." He held up a red medal in the shape of a solo cup.

"Yeah, and it didn't help when you knocked our phone in the bucket of water we were using to practice the relay on Thursday night," Alex said.

"But look, good as new now." J.J. pulled a phone out of his pants' pocket and waved it in front of me.

I glanced back and forth between Alex and J.J.

"It was you," I said. "When I heard the door slam shut on Friday, it wasn't Mr. Snugg or Sandstrom, it was you. You switched out Ella Sandstrom's jewelry, didn't you?"

"We saw Uncle Arthur's note on your desk and..."

"The one that said, 'Meeting David Sandstrom to straighten this out. We need correct jewelry on his wife before tonight,'" I said.

"Yeah, that one. We figured you needed help and she needed some nice jewelry to be buried in. So, we grabbed some from that box you had in your office."

"That box contains the possessions that your Aunt Regina left behind. Why would you put them on Ella Sandstrom?"

"We're sorry, Mel. This week was the first week Uncle Arthur had us help him. It used to be Aunt Regina. We dressed three bodies." J.J. held up three fingers.

"The Schalmer woman on Tuesday, Harriet Carter on Thursday, and Ella Sandstrom." With the Carter file and the Sandstrom file laid out on my desk side by side, my eyes scanned the deceased's belongings' lists.

"It's a lot of work," Alex said.

I stood up and did a quick shimmy shake. "I know where the real jewels are!" I shouted towards Snugg's office up the stairway. "Alex and J.J. put them on Harriet Carter."

"What?" said Snugg, coming to the landing.

"The elderly woman buried on Thursday, the morning of Ella Sandstrom's first viewing. You know! The nursing home sent her over. Her last wishes were a "proper burial.""

"So, Harriet Carter had a dignified, proper burial and was laid to rest with $300,000 in jewelry around her neck," said Snugg in disbelief, shaking his head at Alex and J.J., who stared back, horrified.

"I'll order the backhoe, Mr. Snugg, and…from now on, jewelry is my job."

The twins and Arthur Snugg vigorously nodded in agreement.

Lucky for me and Ms. Harriet Carter, I keep meticulous records of burial plots. ♥

I bet my dad is looking down from heaven and laughing that I traded my career in Pittsburgh for the "deadly dull job" of working for our hometown funeral parlor and his old best friend. And he'd be right. Since I showed up, there's been a lot of dead, but it is anything but dull.

This New Job's Murder

It all started three months ago when I left Grant, my ex, who took the words "love thy neighbor" literally. Everything I owned fit into "Clifford," my fifteen-year-old rusty red RX8 Mazda, except my one-of-a-kind glass block table and our jointly owned thirty-gallon saltwater fish tank. The fish were technically mine, but the visual of Grant watching fish instead of our large screen TV made the choice an easy one.

As I drove across the Fort Pitt Bridge, I waved goodbye to those yinzers in the city. I knew I'd miss their Pittsburghese, the Pirates baseball team, and especially the taco truck parked outside my condo every Tuesday. But here I am. Back in the town I grew up in. It's a little over a two-hour drive away, but Pleasantview is another universe. For example, the clock outside the courthouse is stuck at six. Not sure if it is a.m. or p.m., but either way, time has definitely stopped here.

One of the things that won't stop, however, is the phone at The Peaceful Rest Funeral Home and Cemetery where I now work. It's always ringing. It has become prime real estate in the last few weeks since I started working there. I don't want to brag, but none of it would have been possible without me, Melody Shore. I'm a twenty-eight-year-old paralegal turned funeral assistant. I took the job to help the director, Arthur Snugg. I bet my dad is looking down from heaven and laughing that I traded my career in Pittsburgh for the "deadly dull job" of working for our hometown funeral parlor and his old best friend. And he'd be right. Since I showed up, there's been a lot of dead, but it is anything but dull.

"Peaceful Rest Funeral Home and Cemetery, this is Melody Shore. How may I help you?" With my free hand, I smoothed the Peter Pan collar down on my candy-pink blouse.

"No, sir. I'm sorry, we don't have a members-only mausoleum." I tried not to slam the phone down. Seriously, some of these calls.

I stared out beyond my fishbowl office, with solid glass walls reaching to the fourteen-foot ceiling above. The modern enclosure is a stark contrast to the lamp-lit walls, woodwork, and couches all drowning in shades of beige. I'd like to think that my design sense could make a big difference in updating this place, if I could get Snugg to see the need for it. Thank God for the person who went wild and threw in abalone throw pillows, the only color in the room except for the towering white peace lily—almost a color, if you count its green leaves.

Glass walls and no door meant Arthur Snugg was in clear view when he strode in. Dressed in his standard gray suit and tie, he'd added a light purple shirt instead of his regular white. I smelled a lunch date.

"I haven't properly thanked you." He cleared his throat. "Your smart reasoning skills tracked down the Sandstrom's jewels. You saved me from a three-hundred-grand insurance claim." He laid a folder on my desk.

"That's a compliment I'll take." I smiled, busily typing an invoice. He didn't mention that I single-handedly brought down a murderer who killed a diamond of the community and nearly iced us too.

The printer spit out a fax containing Nina Domenski's insurance papers. Snugg handed them to me without reviewing them.

"Well, I think it's a win for both of us," I said, straightening the file.

"You know, your dad would be proud of you." Snugg spread the new Morris file out on my desk.

"Thanks Mr. Snugg. Proud of us, I think. I can't believe it's been over twelve years already since Mom and I were here for his funeral."

Snugg blinked and cleared his throat. "Allergies," he croaked. His gray eyebrows furrowed; he ran a hand through his slicked black hair.

One reason Snugg hired me: He finally admitted he couldn't run the funeral home without his wife. When they divorced, she arranged to keep all their valuable assets and he got the funeral home.

"You got a new shirt! I like it," I said, quickly changing the subject.

"It's all the new clients. I thought I'd update my look." Snugg adjusted his tie. A bachelor in search of love. His office door could be replaced with a revolving door for the number of women who went through it. For some crazy reason, I respected him anyway. Maybe it was his non confrontation-al way of handling problems, or maybe he reminded me of my dad, cool and calm as a veteran relief pitcher.

"Speaking of updates…" I jumped up so quickly in my wedge sandals that I dove towards the mail on the file cabinet but landed on Snugg instead.

"I've been meaning to ask you," I stepped back and smoothed out my daring red midi skirt. "There's a great sale on remodeling and windows at DJ's. If you book this week, you'll get baseball tickets to three upcoming games, including the opener." I handed him a brochure.

"Ah. Pirates or Bats?"

"Bats. Minor-league tickets. You know, gotta buy local."

"Yes, I looked at it briefly. But we've just had the exterior stone repaired. If the salesperson stops back, tell them not this year."

"But Mr. Snugg, I mean, is this the kind of funeral home people expect nowadays? It's sort of colorless except for the stained glass. I feel like I'm in church and should repent for my sins."

"Hmm. And that's a bad thing?"

I smirked, stifling a laugh.

"Speaking of teams, listen to me carefully. Everything you need for the Morris family at one o'clock is here in this folder." Arthur Snugg tapped the file. "Bob Morris will be arriving shortly. I have a director's meeting in Pittsburgh, so you're up to bat." He chuckled lightly. "Alex and J.J. are in the basement if you need them."

Alex and J.J. are Arthur Snugg's nephews by marriage. Their antics were probably cute in high school, but at twenty-something–

I shook my head. A baseball game would do Snugg good. My Dad and I never missed a game.

"I have the boys cleaning up the storage room. Keep an eye on them. If they finish early, send them outside to work on the grounds. I'll keep my phone on if you need me."

"Don't worry about anything." I waved him away.

A half-hour later, I was just about to call my new boyfriend, Russell, when the front doors opened. I shivered, and the hair on the back of my neck stood up. A broad-shouldered man with sunglasses entered and walked straight into my office.

"Bob Morris. The coroner brought my wife, Denise, yesterday. I am here to finalize arrangements."

He planted his beefy fake-tan frame down in the chair across from me. His wrinkled peach-colored cotton dress shirt was slightly sweaty with freshly smeared lipstick on its collar. He either didn't know how to do laundry or had wasted no time getting back in the game. He tapped his feet impatiently as his orange fingers scrolled through his phone's feed.

"I'm Melody Shore, Mr. Morris. I'm the assistant here at the funeral home and I'll be helping you with your wife's arrangements. I'm sorry for your loss." I stood up and held out my hand. "First, can I offer you something to drink before we get started?"

Bob Morris glanced up over the rim of his sunglasses, half-heartedly shook my hand, and went back to scrolling, then smiled and murmured an answer to the private text on his phone.

Eight weeks of working here had taught me that grief and a grieving spouse don't come with a playbook. I gently asked again, "Can I offer you coffee?"

With no response, I could only sit back down and type up some invoices from the day before. I'd wait.

After a minute, Bob Morris looked up and shoved his phone into his pocket. "Do you have some papers or something I need to sign?"

"Yes. I have your paperwork here, but first we need your decision on several items. One is a casket. We have several that would be just right for your wife. Please, if you'll follow me, we have a display room to help you select the one that you prefer."

"I'm really in a hurry. Do you have a pamphlet or something instead? I mean, they all look the same, don't they? Just a box?"

"Well, sort of. Most people do like to look at the choices in person, because they are different up close. But I believe I have some pamphlets from our provider here on file." I pulled a slightly crumpled one from the very back of my bottom desk drawer.

When I stood up, I caught my reflection in the TV screen behind Bob

Morris—the big one we kept on hand for memorial videos. I looked irritated. I was fit and fleshy—shoulder-length brown hair, and eyes that took in everything in a room in two split seconds. But I couldn't hide my displeasure. Never could. What is it with this guy? He can't take ten minutes to pick out a casket for his wife? I adjusted my face—I had to give him my sales face, didn't I?

Bob flipped the pamphlet in his hands roughly. I wanted to snatch it back and say, Hey, we've only got one of those, but I smiled a plastic smile instead.

"It's more for our use," I said. "Just ignore the markings on the sheet. I've never actually had anyone pick solely from a picture."

"Okay, this one." He flipped through looking only at prices until his carrot-colored finger pointed to the mid-grade casket. "I don't believe in wasting my money. This is the price for the total package, correct? Everything included?"

"Yes." I slid the price sheet and a company pen across the desk in front of him. "One more thing," I said after he signed. "We have several vault choices."

"Vault? What's that? I got the casket. You said that was the whole package. What else could she possibly need? She's already d…"

"Each burial plot requires a vault. Your wife will need a burial vault to line the grave."

"That's not included?"

"A vault is what we use before placing the casket in the ground, so it doesn't sink. It is mandatory, Mr. Morris, and required by us from the state. We have several types."

Ten seconds later, he picked the cheapest—our single reinforced basic concrete vault—no surprise. He stood to leave.

"Can I offer you our customary tour of the grounds?" I was pressing him, yeah, but he was starting to bug me. Didn't he care at all how his wife was buried? "Many families like to choose the exact plot. I can drive you around to show you the best of our open selections." I stood up and grabbed the car keys for the beige Peaceful Rest PT Cruiser and followed him to the front door.

"This spot here." Bob pointed to a circle that marked one of three storm drains on my gravesite map. "That one is fine. I will have my secretary send you the form for the engraving. I can tell you now, it will just say 'Morris.' At a hundred per letter, that's all I'm good for. Now, I'm late for another appointment." Grabbing his keys from his pocket, he pushed past me and headed out the front door.

"But what day do you want for her viewing? And um, sir, we need to do the wording for the newspaper too…Mr. Morris?"

"No viewing, and free paper notice," he said over his shoulder. "Let me know when it's done."

I let the door slam behind him with a bang. I stomped back to my office, grabbed the Domenski bill and stamped it "filed" hard enough to wake the dead. After the jarring echo through the foyer died, I took a few deep breaths.

I opened Denise Morris's file and read the coroner's report. I don't know what I expected, but I was sure there would be half a dozen clues that something was suspicious about Denise's death. I scanned the three-page report. Holy heck! I needed to call Russell!

"Hey, beautiful," Russell McCormick's thick voice answered on the first ring.

"Hey. I needed to hear your voice and ask you a few questions," I said, in what I hoped was a nonchalant tone. It had been two months, and I still felt like a schoolgirl when he answered the phone on or off duty, at the Pleasantview Police Department.

"You know you wouldn't know my voice at all if you hadn't shown up at one of my stakeouts," Russell said. "Who would have thought a beautiful woman would show up snooping around while I was undercover?"

I tried not to picture his ripped body and sexy smile so I could get back to the case file. Six feet of testosterone with a capital T and waves of curly hair—that was Russell. The thoughts didn't help my concentration.

"Speaking of cases," I stammered. "The strangest thing happened here today. Bob Morris just left from making his wife's arrangements. Or, I should say, lack of arrangements."

"You got to meet the philandering Bob Morris. Did he try to make a move?"

"Yuck! No, but I got the creepiest vibe from him. So, I looked at the coroner's report and that's why I'm calling. The coroner's report said the cause of death was blunt force trauma from a fall. It's crazy! Where did she fall, and what did she fall on? They didn't do an autopsy!"

"Mel, I'm sorry you had to deal with Bob Morris of all people, but I'm super-busy. Can we talk tonight? How about dinner and some dancing at The Mountain?" Russell's voice was deep with just the right amount of gravel and suggestion.

"Can't you tell me anything?"

"Ok, just the outline. Denise Marie Morris, age forty-five. Daughter of Ray and Marie Battle, giants of the sporting goods industry and..."

"Owners of everyone's favorite, three-time champions, Pleasantview Bats' baseball team!"

"You got it, slugger. See you tonight!"

"Okay, can't wait."

But it was bugging me—the Morris thing. So I did what any amateur sleuth would do. I did an internet search.

Denise Marie Morris, age forty-five. There it was. She was a member of one of the wealthiest families in town. Money. Big money. I stood up and paced, what was becoming my usual round. Twenty-five steps to the curtained foyer window, peer out, then down to the Lilac Room threshold, walk back through the foyer to the Rose Room entrance, then circle back to my office. So why didn't Bob Morris want to spend any money? Maybe the Battle family knew how to play hardball. Shutting out the son-in-law, Bob Morris? Was that it? Nothing added up.

I was about to look for some county records when the phone rang.

"Peaceful Rest Funeral Home..." I said in my best customer service tone.

"Hello, dear!" My mom's bright voice echoed over the line.

"Pretty busy, Mom. Can I call you back?"

"Now this will just take a minute. I've just learned that Joey Steele is single again, and…"

"What? I don't want a blind date! You know I'm dating someone already. I told you that."

"Dear, you work at a funeral home. Most of the men who you meet don't even have a pulse."

"Very funny, Mother. I've got to go—I'm researching something odd about the last body that came in…wait. Did you know Denise Morris?"

"Denise 'Batty' Morris? Yes, I remember when she married Bob Morris. Her third marriage after two other failed ones. Some women can't keep a man." My mom cleared her throat.

I groaned. "What are you trying to say, Mom?"

"Nothing! Denise made quite a catch with Bob Morris, that's all. He's a looker. I heard my friends at Dawn's Cut and Color say that he was a merchandise manager for AstroTurf before Batty moved in with him. I was tempted to date him myself."

"Gross, Mom. He was horrible."

"You could learn from a man of such stature. Remember, dear, if you work hard, you might find a nice guy like Joey Steele. I can call his mom right now and set it up."

"Gee, thanks, Mother. I should go wallow in my lunch now."

"Anytime, Honey. I'm meeting Marsha at the café for lunch."

"Bye, Mom." My stomach rumbled. Lunch was way late.

Just then something caught my eye on the Bats' team website. Denise had been Vice President of Operations in charge of marketing for the team and apparently forever, practically since she was out of college.

I ran to the fridge, grabbed my raspberry vinaigrette salad from Marsha's Café—my mom's best friend's café and a little neighborhood joint I frequented—and ran back to my desk. While I wolfed down my lunch, still scrolling at my screen, I heard a clatter on the stairs. The noise told me the boys were either done with their task or had given up.

"Hey, Mel, J.J. and I are going for lunch. You want anything?" Alex's voice echoed in the foyer. Alex was burly, short, thick-waisted with a mop of black hair that fell over his eyes. His brother, J.J., was tall and thin and delicate-looking, with a fresh buzz cut of blondish hair. The guy barely ever talked. How these two were twins was beyond me.

"You boys really getting lunch or are you going for beer and lottery tickets again?"

"We're one ticket away from taking on Hollywood! Nyuk, nyuk, nyuk." Alex poked J.J. in the eyes like he was Curly from the Three Stooges.

"As actors? Say, I think Looney Toons is hiring for a remake." They stood there grinning stupidly, and I waved them on. "No thanks, guys, I don't want a liquid lunch."

"It's not all liquid. There are free pretzels," Alex yelled out as they left.

Seconds later the security monitor lit up, showing the lower-level door was open. Alex and J.J. ran through the parking lot toward Mickey's, their favorite bar.

At 4:22, I got ready to close up for the day. I had contacted the proper channels and copied and filed Denise's life insurance claim. There was so little to arrange. The newspaper had already emailed me acknowledging receipt of her obituary notice. My blood pressure started to go up again thinking about her husband purposely blowing off any memorial service.

I angrily wiped away tears. I would call Russell. He'd know what to do.

"Don't tell me you're cancelling our dinner plans," he said, answering the phone.

"I just feel so sad about poor Denise: Two failed marriages, and one husband who gives me the creeps. What a sad end."

Russell put on his cop voice. "It happens pretty often."

"I know life isn't all rainbows and puppies, Russell, but she died from random blunt force trauma! Why did no one even request an autopsy? The husband seems glad she's gone and there's not even an obituary!"

"So now you're seeing some kind of cover up? I thought I was the police officer in this relationship?"

"Thanks for listening."

"Look. If you feel so strongly, I'll look into it. But I'm sure it must have been cut and dried or I'd have the case file, not you, Melody." His voice was sweet, not critical.

"Well, you might be right, but thanks for looking into it." I sighed loudly. "I'm leaving work now. I'll see you at six thirty."

"Wouldn't miss it!" Russell said.

Outside in the parking lot, my new Jeep waited for me. "Blue Betty," I had named her. She started right up, and I was so thankful. The Jeep—unlike my old clunker—had low mileage, a working radio, and an oil pan that didn't require constant love. I got the down payment from selling a few pieces of the jewelry left to me by Frances Blooming in her will. A sweet ride and I owe it all to a woman I only knew for two days. Senseless-ly murdered, but one heck of a generous, fashionable yoga partner with a heart of gold.

I touched the laminated poem on my dash by Linda Ellis read at Frances Blooming's funeral. I read the poem.

> *I read of a man who stood to speak*
> *at the funeral of a friend.*
> *He referred to the dates on their tombstone*
> *from the beginning to the end.*
> *He noted that first came the date of birth*
> *and spoke of the following date with tears,*
> *But he said what mattered most of all*
> *was the dash between those years.*
> *For it matters not how much we own,*
> *the cars, the house, the cash.*
> *What matters most is how we live*
> *and love and how we spend our dash.*

I turned my radio to 103-WROX and turned onto Pine Street. When I got to my apartment, I smiled. I was living out the definition of adulting, my own car and apartment. Sure, it was only a converted attic over a detached garage—a 300-square-foot, one bedroom, no-pets-allowed studio apartment, but the rent was cheap. Plus, the landlord said I could use the garage in the winter.

As I pulled into the driveway, an announcement came on the radio:

"The Pleasantview Bats, owned by the local Battle family, are holding tryouts for a mascot tomorrow at two pm! Come on down, show us your skills, earn some extra cash and be part of the team!"

Wow. I could use the money, and I could see some games! A two for one! I threw my arms up to the left and right like a cheerleader. If I got it, I could see the inner workings of the team and meet the players. And a little cash meant I could pay off Blue Betty faster. The Jeep payment was a tad higher than I expected.

Wait. Would this be a conflict of interest? Surely creepy Bob Morris wouldn't have anything to do with hiring the mascot position at the Bats' stadium, would he?

No. That was ridiculous. An easy gig. I had a real chance at this! I should go for it. My choreographed dance skills were nonexistent, but maybe I could freestyle and be enthusiastic. As I jumped from Blue Betty, did a shoulder shake dance move, and ran up the stairs, a question hit me. What would Russell think?

My new ruggedly handsome boyfriend wouldn't care. It couldn't hurt a girl's eyes to enjoy guys in baseball uniforms. Right?

I dressed in my favorite soft stretchy v-neck, ripped washed jeans, and my black leather Stuart Weitzman heels. To make my lips kissable, I used my favorite Pink Passion lip liner. I added some vintage jewelry purchased from my favorite boutique, Claire's Cottage. The downer of having to move home was mostly erased by the fact that my high school best friend, Claire, owned a vintage dress shop downtown.

I heard the truck drive up. It was Russell, right on time at exactly six thirty. I opened the door as he took the stairs two at a time. His pressed oxford shirt, open at the throat, was paired with casual khakis. His brown wind-tossed hair begged me to push it off his forehead.

He whistled softly. "You're smokin, Mel."

"Ha ha. Thanks, so are you."

He reached for my hand and escorted me to his Ford F-150. A pop station played on the radio. As I buckled my seatbelt, I leaned toward him and took a selfie.

"I'm starving." My stomach provided a supporting rumble.

"Me too." He gave a deep throaty chuckle then hummed along to the radio as he drove.

The Mountain was an old stone inn that sat at the top of a hill overlooking Pleasantview. It's now a restaurant that serves the best wings around, and on Friday nights there's a live band. Wood-beamed, hardwood floors, leather booths—cozy.

"Do you know who the band is tonight?" I asked.

"Some country rock band, I think." After we were seated with our rolls, Russell buttered me a roll and then said, "See that guy on your left?"

"The one with the pretty girlfriend eating everything in sight and nervously glancing out the window?"

Russell smirked. "First date, paranoid weed smoker."

"Ha ha. Always a police angle on the story," I said, sipping my sangria. "Speaking of a police angle, is anyone investigating Denise Morris's death?"

"There's nothing to learn. It was an accident. End of story…" He reached over to hold my hand.

I pulled away. "Nothing to learn? I mean, come on!"

Even in the dark lighting, I saw Russell's eyes narrow. Then he sighed. "As far as the police department knows, she committed suicide. It's a shame. A successful woman, but I guess money doesn't buy happiness."

"Bob Morris doesn't seem at all to care that his wife is gone!" I took a big bite of my roll, chewing hard.

"He's a jerk and nothing but trouble." His eyes went wide, maybe a little pleading in them. "Look—Melody—"

"Don't worry, Russell, I've seen men like Bob Morris before."

"I know, and I hate to say it, Melody, but trouble seems to find you. Just do me a favor and stay the hell away from the guy, okay?"

I silently hoped I wouldn't see Bob tomorrow at my audition at the stadium. Should I tell Russell? No. Not yet.

The server returned with our main course. After dinner, as the second upbeat number began, Russell grabbed my hand. "Great song. Do you want to dance?"

Russell had me by the fingertips and was on his feet and in the middle of the crowded dance floor before I could say anything. We edged past several pairs of twirling couples and then he pulled me into his arms.

"Did I tell you, you look smokin' tonight, Ms. Shore. I hope I don't have to arrest you for arson." He nuzzled my ear, then slipped his hand down to the small of my back in a very suggestive way. Whew! I needed some ice water.

Saturday morning, I awoke to the aroma of strawberry pancakes and the lingering scent of sandalwood on my sheets.

After breakfast, Russell headed to work, and I quickly cleaned up the dishes and took a shower.

Before I got dressed for the day I couldn't help calling him.

"Sorry to call you at work, but I forgot to mention that I'm headed to the stadium this morning and..."

"What? Which stadium?" He was using his cop voice.

"Bats." Why did I call and blurt that out? My mom always said I have a mouth like a freight train.

"Why are you going to the stadium? Don't tell me Arthur Snugg is advertising in the programs now."

"Ha ha. I'm going to buy a ticket. I love baseball and miss going to the games with my dad."

"I know you do, Mel," his voice softened back to a low rumble. "We could go to a game–we should go."

"That would be amazing." My heart skipped a beat. I looked around for my purse and keys.

"Oh...hold that thought, Melody, I gotta go, the chief is calling. Call me afterwards. And please watch your back, okay? For me."

"Russell?"

Too late, he disconnected. Was that watch your back and don't trip in your vintage shoes or don't mess with a murder?

I arrived early to tryouts expecting a large lineup of men and women who love the Pleasantview Bats' baseball team, just like me. A single printed sign "Tryouts Today" hung from a post in the grass. My heart was beating fast as I walked through the red brick pillar archway marking the entrance to the stadium and field. Together, my dad and I had watched them break ground when they built the place. It had been a strip mall, but now it was a stadium that had the capacity of about 3,400 for baseball and approximately 4,000 for a concert venue. It could almost seat the entire town. Along the paved pathway, a flagpole proudly displayed a large American flag, and overhead team banners waved in the light breeze. Another sign, *Tryouts This Way*, directed me down a ramp to the stadium's basement. Offices, locker rooms, and meeting rooms. I glanced up at the right-field bleacher seats as I went past. My favorite section in the whole stadium. My Dad and I used to sit in Section 202.

At the bottom of the ramp, a loosely hung chain blocked the entrance. Beyond it I saw a hallway door marked, simply, *Tryouts.*

"Hello? Anyone?" I called out over the chain.

No one answered.

A small running start and I jumped over the low hanging link chain that was drawn across the doorway. I was pretty proud of myself until I entered the room. The place was almost empty.

"Do they hold tryouts on varying days?" I asked the guy wearing a ninety dollar Nike warm-up suit who was doing what appeared to be ballet moves.

"No." He stopped pirouetting. "This is the only tryout," he said, touching his toes effortlessly.

I looked around. The room was plain—pipes above along the cement-block ceiling, a flattened indoor-outdoor carpet, some bare tables and chairs pushed into a corner. Five people were trying out. Me, Twinkle-toes, another guy on his smartphone, and two others who were busy taking selfies and drinking cups of water from a water cooler sitting nearby. I was going to stand out like a foul ball. And who was judging this thing? It was supposed to start at two. Where was everybody?

I waited. The temperature reading on the thermometer mounted on the wall read seventy-four degrees Fahrenheit—warm for the lower level of a stadium.

Two o'clock came and went. No one showed up to interview us. Two of the guys were doing a choreographed routine. Twinkle-toes was doing a backbend, and the last guy was still on his phone.

Ten minutes later, star player and two-time MVP Samuel Rodriguez arrived. He was dressed in his practice uniform and, in stark contrast, carried a briefcase. The other applicants didn't react, but my eyes were as big as saucers, being so close to one of my heroes.

"That's Samuel Rodriguez! He's the best right fielder our team has ever had," I whispered reverently to Twinkle-toes. "He looks hot."

Twinkle-toes gave a disgusted look, turned his back to me and walked twenty feet away. Me and my mouth again.

Rodriguez carried an old-school boombox, which he set down on a small table and plugged in. "It's a Beautiful Day for a Ball Game" blasted out of the speakers.

"I love this song!" I said as I swayed along to the music. The other tryouts stood silently as we all watched him pull a stack of papers from the briefcase.

"These are preliminary waivers that need to be filled out right now," he shouted to the group. "Then I will audition one at a time."

I was not as flexible as Twinkle-toes, but I came prepared. I rushed to the table. When I turned around from filling out the form, the others were standing behind me. I guess I was the only one carrying a pen.

"Never mind, let's move on," Rodriguez said, waving us back. "If you signed in with your name and number, that's enough."

The guys stepped away from the table and formed a line in front of me. Drat, I'm now last in line.

"Okay, so I don't know how they corralled me into choosing the team mascot, but what the hell. Let's just say—well, I'm not always…yeah, let's just say I owed them one." He laughed, loudly.

We didn't.

His face went serious. "Okay. So, tell me a little about yourselves and uh, do whatever you'd do as the team mascot."

Twinkle-toes stepped forward. Although he didn't want to talk to me earlier, he sure could speak now. "I danced most of my life. Crowds and young children don't really bother me," he said, moving to the music. This guy did have rhythm, I'll give him that.

That's when I felt my stomach drop. What was I doing here? What did I think tryouts for a mascot would be? A ten-minute interview about whether I like mustard and onion on my hotdog, and asking if I've ever caught a fly ball before the bounce? Let one of these guys take the job. I needed a quick exit.

Next, the cell phone guy questioned Rodriguez about the salary and hours rather than the apparent prerequisite performance.

"I'm not the one to ask that." Rodriguez frowned. "Next."

The two guys who were doing selfies were a team effort with a practiced act. They didn't dance or jump. They acted out a mime routine with one guy acting as a baseball patron and the other the mascot escorting him to his seat—their prop, a folding chair they found somewhere. Their routine was followed by an elaborate air high-five.

"Next," Rodriguez shouted. My palms started to sweat. "Wait," Rodriguez said. "I totally forgot the costume. I apologize. Bob Morris couldn't be here. Hold on. I will be right back."

"Oh, great, Bob Morris."

The four guys turned to look at me. Oops, did I say that out loud?

Rodriguez appeared several minutes later, dragging a large, black rubber bag. On a closer look, I realized the bag was a suit with wings. He stepped back six feet to a closet attached to the wall, pulled the latch, then opened the door, lifting a smiling bat head from the top shelf. The thing had pointed ears and two orange feet.

"This is Batter," he shouted, demonstrating how the flexible lining in the feet allowed them to stretch over shoes. "I forgot to tell you, but you need to be comfortable in this if you're going to work this gig. So, you might as well put it on," he said with a grin, suddenly dropping the suit in front of me.

I stared down at the rubber suit.

Five guys stared expectantly at me. Although I had no intention of taking off any of my clothes to put on the costume, they gawked at me.

"I'll use the locker room, Coach," I said, flashing a smile.

Around the corner, I debated my choices. Keep the costume and run straight out of the stadium and never come to another game again—or put on the suit. Wait, I was the only one who filled out my contact info. Drat. Okay, put on the suit then.

In the locker room, I felt giddy seeing all the guys' names on their cubbies, even some clean uniforms ready for Opening Night. My fingers traced over Rodriguez's nameplate and the first baseman's nameplate. I snapped a few pictures and took selfies in front of their cubbies. Why not? Surely, once they saw me in the costume, I would never be in here again, unless I was in the cheap seats, a non-name customer, just like I always was.

It was now or never. I pulled the rubber suit over my head. It looked like a barrel made of black licorice and smelled like the wrestling mats from a high school gym. The wings made it hard to move my arms to put on the feet. I couldn't sit down because of the wings, so I pulled off the suit and put the feet on first. I was sure bats had small feet, but this suit's feet were big. Somehow, I put the suit on again, then lifted the large head and let it fall over my shoulders. I was dressed.

In the tryout room, I heard the music crank up with a pump-up-the-crowd song they usually played at the stadium when a home run hitter came up to bat. My vision was limited to straight ahead. Russell had said, "Watch your back," but if there was someone knocking people off at the stadium, I wouldn't be able to see if anyone was next to me, let alone behind me. I silently prayed that I wouldn't break anything, including myself, then bounded across the locker room and around the bend out into the tryout area.

"Batter up," I yelled. It came out as a mumble under the large, padded head. Raising my winged arms and using my best line-dance moves, I swooped across the room bouncing from the balls of my Big Bird feet to my toes. The weight of the suit accidentally propelled me straight into the wall. My left wing caught on something. My head hit something hard. A lot of loud crashing came from behind me, and I started to slide around as if I was on roller skates. What the hell? Was I stepping on bats? A whole barrelful of them?

This wasn't going as planned. What would Russell think if he saw me? My large feet kept rolling on the bats and propelled me forward like a box on a conveyor belt straight into the four gawk-eyed men. I couldn't help it. I wasn't sure who I landed on, but I seemed to have knocked them over like bowling pins.

I sat stunned for a while until Twinkle-toes gently removed my bat head.

"Thanks," I said. "Guess I should have waited for sound waves to bounce back before I flew forward."

No one laughed.

I wrenched the rubber suit from my body right there, kicked off the feet, and looked around for my purse.

Samuel Rodriguez was doubled over in silent laughter. Then he picked up a couple of bats, shut off his boombox, and shoved the stack of papers back into his briefcase. "Way to bowl over your competition," he said. "Yeah, we've got enough for us to decide. I have your contact info. We'll be in touch. Thanks." He walked out of the room, with a quick wink in my direction.

My face flushed. I really wanted to run out after him and steal his phone in case he had taken a video.

Outside in the parking lot it was pouring rain. Covering my head with the hood on my coat, I crossed the street in a dash for Blue Betty. I ran right into Bob Morris. He stumbled backward and his designer sunglasses flew off and crunched under his feet.

"Oh, crap!" I muttered, turning quickly away.

"Wait. Do I know you?" His face turned red.

"Excuse me, Mr. Morris. It was totally an accident. Melody Shore. I work at The Peaceful Rest Funeral Home and Cemetery."

"Did I forget to sign something?" he said, his eyebrows knotting up.

"No, no, I was…well actually, I was trying out for your team mascot."

"You're the female applicant. Rodriguez just called about you." His face cleared.

"News travels fast…I truly apologize for uh…your glasses and, uh, tryouts ending…early."

"I can buy new ones. Come on back inside so we can talk." He looked me up and down. "So you want to be our bat, huh?"

I nodded.

"Well, I don't think you can stand much more rain for today without your waterproof wings." He laughed a little too loudly at his own joke.

"Wait, me? I got the job?"

"Yes, you did. On Rodriguez's recommendation," he said earnestly.

We walked to the nearby double-wide aluminum-sided trailer labeled "Administrative Offices," and he held open the door.

Bob Morris's office was as small as mine at the funeral home, except he had pieces of grass turf rather than lilies inside. Promotional water bottles, empty coffee cups, and two corn curl bags littered his desk. Rain echoed off the metal roof.

"Excuse my mess." He cleared a pile of T-shirts off a chair so I could sit.

After a few minutes, somehow, Bob Morris talked up the idea of working for the Bats. I would be a great asset to their program, he insisted. He piled up a gift bag with several promotional hoodies, T-shirts, and a water bottle. The pay would be a flat per-game appearance of a hundred dollars.

"You sure you want me to take all this?" I hesitated.

"Sure. I'm out of this office next week. Less to take."

"You're moving?"

"Yes, up to the main offices inside the stadium. Upper management offices on the second floor."

"Oh, congratulations."

"I'll be up there if you need anything, anything at all. Don't hesitate to ask."

As he talked, I glanced around his office. No pictures of his wife anywhere. How was this the same guy from yesterday? So friendly. Could he have bamboozled Denise into marrying him for her money?

"Mr. Morris..."

"You can call me Bob."

"Bob, I just wanted to say again how sorry I am about your wife. I'm sure you miss working with her every day."

"Um, yes, I do." He crossed his arms over his thick chest.

"Was the accident here at the stadium?"

Bob Morris picked up a half-empty snack bag and peered in. "She fell, hit her head."

"That's terrible! Do a lot of people fall at the stadium?" The bag of hoodies slid out of my hands and hit the floor with a slap.

"What? No." His eyes bored through me and then he turned to the bag he'd given me, now lying flat on the floor. I assumed his glare meant pick up the hoodies.

"That must have been terrible to witness." I reached down for the hoodies.

"I didn't witness it." He pulled a stack of papers from a drawer and handed them to me.

"Oh?" I asked, as I took the papers.

He stood and moved toward his office door.

"Do they suspect foul play?" I stayed seated.

"Miss Shore, your job is to run a funeral home, not investigate accidents. You think because Rodriguez picked you, you can get involved in our personal matters?" He put a hand out expecting me to give back the unsigned contract.

I didn't. I just sat there and stared at him.

"Look," he said gruffly, "if you want to work here, Melody, stick to entertaining people. Stick to that...and mind your own business."

A-ha. There's the Bob Morris I met back at the funeral home. His hands touched his nose and tugged on his ear, but it wasn't a signal for me to steal home. I suspected Bob Morris was hiding something and the trailer suddenly felt small.

"Yeah, let's bury that. I mean, I will. I mean, I'm sorry. I didn't mean to intrude. Let me sign these papers and I'll be outta here."

Morris stood in the doorway as my signature got a workout. Eight pages, twelve places, including my initials on four more lines.

Morris started babbling about stats and attendance, and it went in one ear and out the other, but I sighed with relief when I heard him say the team mascot didn't travel with the team. Good. It shouldn't interfere with my job at Old Peaceful.

"We have a strict employee policy of not dating the players, so don't get any ideas," he added at the end.

"I've got a boyfriend, so I won't be—"

"Good," he said, still blocking the doorway.

"He's a cop."

Morris's eyes went wide and he stepped back, just long enough for me to bolt past him, my heart beating fast and my legs pumping.

It was a little after four thirty-five when I arrived home. I went straight to my bed and lay down with my feet up on the wall. Bob Morris. Something is wrong, something is up—something weird. I knew it. But I also knew I shouldn't stick my nose in the middle of it. As I scrolled through my phone, I tried to focus on the fact that I, Melody Shore, was the new Pleasantview Bats' team mascot, and I had literally bowled over the competition. Knocked them down—ha! I tried to forget the otherwise embarrassing moments of the afternoon. I saw two missed calls from Russell. An earlier text read, "what r u doing?" with a heart-eyes emoji.

I pushed favorites on my phone and called him.

"Hey, Clutch, I almost sent out an APB on you."

"Clutch?"

"You know. Our first date. When you saved yourself from an attacker with your clutch?"

"Okay, that wasn't a date. That was a funeral. And you mean my Betsy Johnson vintage clutch. And don't forget the lipstick and shoes." I laughed. "Okay. I get it. I guess I am also good in a clutch situation."

"Where you been? Everything okay?"

"Yes, everything is great. Crazy workday. You should have seen…" I stopped mid-sentence.

"Did you get your ticket? Out at the stadium?"

"Oh…uh—well—I…."

I definitely couldn't tell him about the mascot position now. He wasn't going to like me working for Bob Morris. What if this Morris case was the one keeping Russell so busy, but he couldn't tell me? I mean, Denise Morris's fall just didn't seem like an accident. If it wasn't, then my number one suspect was Bob Morris, my new boss. Maybe he was Russell's biggest suspect, too? I glanced at the pile of promo items Morris had given me stacked neatly in my closet.

"Melody?"

"Russell, do you think it's true that people kill others for one of three reasons?"

"What?"

"You know, money, love, or revenge?"

"I don't know, Mel. I think it's way more complicated than that. But those three top my list."

I reached over to my nightstand for the water bottle Bob Morris gave me.

"Melody, what did you go to the stadium for?"

The water bottle slipped from my hand. "Russell, I just spilled water everywhere. I need to get a towel…maybe I'll just shower."

"If you want me to come over and help you take that shower, I will gladly volunteer for the job."

"If I need help, you'll be the only one I call."

"I'm at your service, and should you need help, a towel is optional," he said in a low voice.

As soon as we disconnected, my phone buzzed again.

"I'm not in the shower yet," I said into the phone.

"Hi, it's Samuel Rodriguez, and that's a shame."

"I didn't mean…Oh, forget it. Samuel, how did you get my number?"

"You wrote down your contact info, remember?"

"Is everything still okay with the mascot position?" I paced the room.

"Oh, yeah, that's fine. I'm calling about tomorrow night."

"Tomorrow night? The game isn't till Thursday." I confirmed on my calendar that Thursday was the day I'd marked with a large star and smiley face.

"I'm free, though. So I can come over, right?"

"Over where?"

"Your apartment."

"My apartment?" I slammed the closet door shut. I'd just met the guy.

"Look, Samuel, I'm not available. Sorry."

"I'll come Wednesday then. We can get to know each other better."

"Wednesday? No, I am not available Wednesday, or any other night. I have a boyfriend."

"Yeah, well—"

"I'm serious."

"I was just being friendly. Listen, Mary, your mascot job is thanks to me. Do yourself a favor and keep your head in the costume and your mouth shut."

What the hell was he talking about? Had Morris gotten to him already?

"Listen, if this is what the job is—"

Rodriguez laughed, kind of wound up and tight, like sharp dog barks.

"Just kidding around with you, Mary. Ha, ha. We're all good, right?"

"It's Melody."

"Sure, whatever," Rodriguez said, and hung up.

"You thickheads!" Snugg screamed at Alex and J.J. "You both need to come with me right now. We're late. New landscaping service, did you forget?"

Snugg turned on a dime, speaking calmly as he turned to me. "Melody, I need these prearrangement brochures updated with the new pricing this morning." Arthur Snugg was at his best on Monday mornings.

I would tell Snugg later about the second job. After all, it was only seasonal and wouldn't conflict with Old Peaceful.

Around noon, the double wooden doors to the funeral home pushed open and Denise Morris entered. I'd seen her inert and lifeless body in the basement of the funeral home and had seen her photograph on a dozen different websites. I was frozen in horror as she extended her manicured hand. I couldn't shake it as one of my hands had a death grip on my desk and the other was planted on my chest feeling for my heartbeat.

"Melody," she sang out.

"Yes. Can I help you?" I whispered to the ghost in front of me. Maybe I'd been working too hard. Digi Filing all the old records from past years when I should have taken walks and got a manicure...the ghost had nice nails, cherry red.

"I'm sorry, I should have called first. I am Sheila Battle. Denise's sister... Twin sister."

"Sheila." Her name blew out of my mouth like an expelling balloon. "I am so very sorry for your loss."

"Thank you," she said, a slight waver in her voice. "If it's okay, I really don't want to discuss my sister. It's still too raw."

"Sure...What can I help you with?"

"I'm wondering, do you have some time to talk about your new position?"

The funeral home was silent except for the whispers of Alex and J.J., who I could see peeking around the corner of the Lilac Room.

"I can take lunch now." I grabbed my purse from my desk drawer, stepped out of my office and in ten steps, held the front door for Sheila.

"Guys, if your uncle needs me, I'm taking lunch. Cover for me." I didn't wait for their answer.

Sheila unlocked the door to her BMW X5 and motioned for me to get in.

"I really appreciate this on such short notice. I wanted to go over a few things," she said, starting the keyless ignition. "Your choice. Where do you want to go for lunch?"

"How about the Corner Cupboard?" I said. The Corner Cupboard had been around ever since I could remember, and it had never been updated. An authentic diner on the corner of Main and Fifth Street, in the center of Pleasantview. They served salty fries, juicy hamburgers, and spicy gossip if you sat at the bar during happy hour.

A five-minute drive in Sheila's swanky car and by the time we sat down, I felt like a celeb. A new part-time job, a fabulous time with Russell the past weekend, and now, lunching with one of the Battles. In one weekend, my life was turning around.

We ordered. Burger for me, Cobb salad for her, no dressing.

"That Samuel, he is so funny," Sheila said after taking a quick look at her texts.

"Samuel Rodriguez?" A faint blush rose on my cheeks.

"What other Samuel would there be?"

I averted my eyes and checked out the room. Wood tables, heavy benches, tiny little vases with flowers from somebody's yard, probably. I'd seen it a million times, but I was dodging—I didn't want to talk about Rodriguez with Sheila.

Sheila rambled on. Several times, I thought I caught the screen on her phone light up with texts. From Bob? From Samuel?

Ten more minutes on Rodriguez, the food came, and Shelia was still talking. "...as if Rodriguez isn't enough to make the Pleasantview Bats great..." She flipped her perfectly manicured nails through her hair, smiling.

I had to choke back comments like, He's a douche, and What a slimy jerk. I couldn't tell if she was trying to get me to spill on Rodriguez or just had the hots for him or something. My mind wandered. I swirled my fries in the large mound of ketchup on my plate, as my mind replayed the crazy facts of Denise Morris's death and her heartless husband—technically, my new boss. Wait...and he was the brother-in-law of the woman in front of me. That snapped me back.

"Sheila, about the mascot position. What did you want to talk about?"

"Oh, yes. Melody, this job is just right for you. We're a great group of people to work with. And this job has its perks. I mean, what more can you want besides free tickets and lots of available men?"

"Oh, I'm not looking for a guy." I looked toward the open kitchen and imagined Russell behind the counter cooking pancakes.

"Are we single women ever really looking?" She laughed.

"Sheila, can I ask you something about Denise?"

"My sister? She's dead. Nothing can bring her back. Oh wait, you know that. You guys are going to bury her." Her laugh turned nervous, and she ran her fingers through her salon-perfect hair again.

Something wasn't right and my scalp buzzed.

"I heard it was a suicide. I'm sorry. That must be hard."

"Who told you that?" Shelia's voice went up an octave. Her manicured fingernails tapped the table hard enough that a small fake diamond on her nail popped off onto the table. Alarm bells were definitely ringing now. Was this why she invited me to lunch? To warn me off Rodriguez?

"Bob Morris. Saturday, he said she jumped and hit her head."

Sheila started chomping away at her salad. I was barely touching my burger.

"Bob was with me, working."

"On Saturday?"

"No. The night she fell…from the bleachers," Sheila whispered.

"So, it was an accident? Has the health department come by to check the railings? Are they safe? I mean, I'd hate for a fan to fall, especially a kid."

The waitress was heading our way with a check, and Sheila grabbed it from the waitress's hand and threw a credit card the woman's way.

"Hey—thanks, but I can pay for half—" I said, trying to be nice. My burger had barely three bites out of it.

Sheila smiled like we had just met. "Melody, my sister Denise's death isn't for you to worry about. Safety and security isn't your department, it's ours, and we're covered. Everything is fine. It was just an accident. Everything is safe. You're our new team mascot. That's all. You can stick to your job, and I'll stick to mine."

"Yep. I'm clear on that. That's what Rodriguez said when he called me." I smiled and pursed my lips.

"Samuel called you?" A vein throbbed in her neck.

Sheila clicked her nails on the table, then saw the check sitting there, signed it and chucked the pen on top of it. Poor thing did not know I was testing her. She clicked harder, the acrylic nails making an instant racket. I thought I'd better back down before she broke a nail and blamed me.

"Yeah, he wanted to go over my job duties." I smiled sweetly, strapping my vintage purse across my chest. "Oh, hey, thanks for lunch, too."

She ignored the thank you and went right back to Rodriguez. "Oh, that's right, that's right, he mentioned he hired you for Bob." She instantly relaxed and folded up her napkin. Her phone lit up again and this time I definitely saw the name "Bob" on the screen.

"That Bob, he thinks he can boss me around the way he bossed my sister around," Shelia said as she tossed her phone in her purse.

"Sheila, do you think someone hurt your sister?" I asked as we headed out the door of the Corner Cupboard.

"No, hon. It was an accident," she said as she slid into her BMW. "But I will tell you this. Women shouldn't be pushovers. Denise was a pushover." Sheila put her head in her hands, bending over the steering wheel, suddenly turning on the waterworks. "I should have never been working. She was my sister, and she was all alone."

I couldn't believe her cold, uncaring demeanor could change so suddenly. But everyone grieves differently. It rarely shocked me anymore, the range and drastic switch of emotions human beings came up with. So, I patted her on the shoulder and recited my standard funeral assistant counsel.

"Sheila, family members grapple and exchange harsh words because of stress and grief. You lost a sister, your twin. It's okay to grieve. Bob Morris is grieving too. I wouldn't take what he does personally right now."

"I'm the new head Vice President of Operations. Bob answers to me now. My sister ran herself ragged day and night, making him look like he is a superstar, but he's not. He's full of himself. I mean, he's in charge of the grounds crew, for God's sake! He barely does a thing, and he steals from the vending machines all day long! He lives on junk food."

I clipped my seat belt, trying to sound casual. "What kind of junk food?"

"Corn curls. What grown man eats four or five snack bags of corn curls a day?" She gripped the wheel tightly.

Ah. The answer to the mystery of his strangely orange fingers.

"I bet you really miss your sister. I always wished I had a sister. Someone to talk fashion with. Brothers don't understand."

Sheila popped the Beamer into reverse, suddenly calm. "I do. I miss her."

We were quiet for the five minutes it took to get back to The Peaceful Rest. I tried to gracefully get out of the car, but I must have stepped in gum while leaving the restaurant, and my foot stuck to her monogrammed floor mat. When I exited her car, the mat came with me.

Sheila's face went beet-red in a split second.

"Hey—sorry," I said, unsuccessfully trying to unstick the mat from my shoe.

"That's my mat!" she exclaimed, watching me try to unstick the thing.

"I'm really sorry…I must've stepped in—" I was pulling, but the gum kept sticking. But what I was really doing was watching her face: Fire-red and angry, the way people get over stupid things, when there's something much bigger that they're furious about.

She caught me watching her, then stared at me, blankly. Then: "It's just…"

"What?" The shoe came unstuck.

"Try being a twin in a sporting goods family." She rolled her eyes. "A twin girl."

All at once, Alex and J.J. came out the front door. J.J. addressed me, but his eyes were on Sheila. "Uncle Arthur left in a rush. He has a tooth-ache."

Sheila got out of the Beamer and extended her hand to J.J. "Sheila Battle," she said. "I sincerely apologize for keeping Melody out so long. We had some matters regarding my sister's burial we needed to clear up, and time got away."

I gave her a questioning look. Our lunch conversation was pretty mundane. Why lie about it?

"Here," Sheila Battle reached into her purse. "For both of you gentle-men. You look like baseball fans. Enjoy the game." Sheila turned to me and winked.

"Whoo-hoo! Thanks. Two box seats to this Thursday's game," Alex whooped.

"Hey, that's opening night," J.J. whistled as Sheila drove away. "Melo-dy, you got any more friends with benefits?"

On Wednesday, the phone line was dead at The Peaceful Rest. A branch from the overgrown willow tree in the front lawn had come crashing down overnight. In my office, I was on my cell phone trying to schedule the repairs when Arthur Snugg walked by pushing a casket.

"Melody, did you finish the PowerPoint for Andrew Wilson's memorial?" he asked.

"Done, Mr. Snugg. I even added music." I brought up the memorial slide on my computer. Music and pictures filled my screen.

We silently watched a lifetime go by on my screen. Caught up in the slideshow, I didn't notice Alex and J.J. standing at the edge of my office peering over the parked coffin.

"Awesome job, Melody." They high fived when the slide show ended. Not your typical reaction, but I'm not picky about praise for my hard work.

"Thanks." I stood up. "While you are all here, I want to tell you some news…"

"Uncle Arthur, you need to pay her more," J.J. interrupted. "We don't want her to leave."

"I got a second job but I'm not leaving." I gave Alex and J.J. my best stern look.

"Melody, we can discuss your salary, if there is a problem," Snugg offered. His forehead furrowed and he suddenly crossed his hands over his belly. His funeral pose. Not a good sign if I really had been looking for a raise.

"Actually, I took the job mostly because it seemed like a fun thing to do. I'm the new mascot of the Pleasantview Bats' baseball team. It won't interfere with working here."

"That's why that woman took you to lunch and gave us the tickets. She's your boss," J.J. said like he'd solved a difficult math problem.

"Nice work and nice perks!" Alex chimed in.

"The only perk we can offer here is burial, knock on wood." J.J. knocked on the lid of the shiny walnut coffin. "And no one likes swag with the funeral home name on it."

I laughed. Maybe I was beginning to like the two stooges.

Arthur Snugg sighed heavily. "How many times do I need to remind you two, I am your boss. Remember, you two work for me. You cannot offer raises or swag, whatever that is." He turned to me. "Congratulations, Melody." Snugg showed a rare smile. "I hope you enjoy the side job. I think we should get some tickets after all. Minor league is more fun, right?"

"Hey," Alex said. "Show them the autograph we got when the right fielder showed up looking for Melody."

"Wait, Rodriguez came here?" I clicked off the slideshow, which was starting over, and closed my computer screen.

"Yeah, you're really playing the field," Alex said. "Then when J.J. and I went to lunch over at Mickey's, we saw him again with your foxy baseball boss."

"What a guy," J.J. piped in.

"Yeah, they were all chummy." Alex mimes a kiss with an invisible woman. "Until the guy that was here the other day came up to them and put a stop to it." Alex nudged JJ. "The guy with the tan. What was his name? Bob Mortan?"

"Morris," I said.

"Yeah, that's him."

"Seriously? Did you hear anything they were saying?" I pulled out my tablet and pen.

"No, but it was packed," Alex said. "Maybe they didn't get the right order. Those two were all arguing and stuff. But after our nachos came, I didn't hear anymore."

I wanted to ask more, but the refrigeration repairman arrived, and all four men went down to the morgue for an inspection.

Opening night for the first baseball game of the season finally came. My outfit wasn't vintage, just a long sleeve, lightweight scoop neck, cotton t-shirt, and yoga pants. Even though I would be hot, I didn't want to be itchy. Outside my apartment window, there was a light misty rain and the news meteorologist was forecasting possible thunderstorms later in the evening.

I arrived early at the stadium before the crowds. If Dad could see me now, he'd say, "My girl, a Pleasantview Bat. I couldn't be prouder." Then he'd smile a gigantic smile.

The rain clouds were far off on the horizon, laying low. It was going to be a beautiful evening. Boxes filled with programs laid at the entrance, already unpacked and awaiting ushers to hand them out. I picked up a program and sped down the ramp toward the restricted area section, bouncing up and down like the popping popcorn in the concession stand. Bob had mailed me an employee lanyard and instructions for clocking in earlier in the week. With my stadium pass hanging on a lanyard around my neck, the security guard simply nodded to me as I entered the employees-only section, where I had tried out last weekend.

After clocking in, I ruffled through the program as I headed to the locker room. That's odd. Rodriguez had been scratched for the evening.

And then I saw it. On page two of the program, a full-page ad depicting the bat mascot. Below a cartoon bat picture in small print, it said that I would be in Section 114, handing out free "Bat" hats to all children under twelve. Limited supply only. My first game and excited fans would trample me for free hats. Fabulous.

"Ms. Shore," the guard outside the locker room said as he read the name on my employee pass. "The players are inside. I took your costume upstairs to the women's restroom on the second floor."

"Thank you," I said, biting my lip. "Which way is that?"

He pointed to the executive elevator.

"Oh, upstairs."

Pictures of the stadium were etched into the elevator's interior walls. I rode up to level two and almost skipped down the carpeted hallway. A wood-framed frosted glass door was marked "Women's Restroom." Tiled walls lined the room. A gold-trimmed mirror hung above a vanity and cushioned seat. I couldn't help but sit down to touch up my makeup and fluff my hair, even though no one would see me. There were five stalls and three showers. Very posh.

I dressed in my get-up and headed for Section 114.

Bob Morris had texted that a photo session was scheduled there before the game. I was supposed to pose with the players. But Samuel Rodriguez was standing there, which instantly soured my mood. Luckily, we couldn't make direct eye contact or conversation because of my big bat head.

"Come on! Fly, little bat! Oh-oh-oh...you can't? What's wrong with you?" He guffawed loudly.

"Why don't you jump? Oh, that's right, you can't. Let me guess, pulled groin?" I shouted through my bat head. Well, through the neck actually.

That brought a slightly murderous look into his eyes.

After twenty minutes of photos—which felt eighteen minutes too long for me—it was game time.

When the players cleared out, I saw there were at least one hundred hats for me to give out. I wasn't exactly trampled. Mostly, I handed out hats sedately between the innings.

I waved to the crowd and they waved back. No one rushed toward me, but they did line up to see me, the Pleasantview Bat's mascot. The children were excited by the hats and laughed when I made my wings flap outward as if I was flying or applauding the players.

A game goes by quickly when you're dancing yourself crazy and high-fiving minor league fans like it was an Olympic sport. Sadly, in the eighth inning, the score was zero to six. Fans trickled out starting in the sixth. As dark clouds loomed overhead, everyone except the diehards cleared out by the top of the ninth inning.

After the game, most of the players quickly exited the stadium. I suppose another opening game was old news to them. I was too excited to leave, though. The noise of the game and the cheering fans made me feel like a superstar.

I was sauntering down the lower-level hallway still dressed as a bat, thinking of cool moves for the next game, when I saw Sheila. She waved as she entered the elevator to the upper management offices.

"Melody, you did great tonight." She grinned broadly.

"Thanks, Sheila," I hollered, but she couldn't hear me under the bat head.

I tried to take the head off, but it wouldn't budge. Great. Now what? Everyone was gone.

I ran to the elevator and pressed two for the executive suites. Sheila would probably help me.

When I got off the elevator, voices murmured down the hall.

As I neared the frosted glass door with gold lettering marked "Sheila Battle," I realized the tense voices were coming from her office.

I was about to pull open the door when I heard, "…and another thing. That girl we hired to be the mascot? She was asking a lot of questions."

"What questions?" Sheila asked.

"About Denise." I recognized the other voice. It was Bob Morris.

"She's harmless."

"Yeah, so you say. Your man Rodriguez seems ready to tango with her."

"My man? What do you mean by that?" Sheila snapped.

"I mean, you think Rodriguez actually cares about you? Think again."

"More than you do! Denise this, Denise that. Well, Denise is gone now. I'm in charge!"

Glass shattered. Then Bob screamed.

I flattened myself to the wall in the hallway, keeping my bat wings as still as I could. They were heavy, though, and it took all my willpower to stand in place.

"What's the matter with you? Stay away from me. You did something to her, didn't you?" Bob's voice quavered.

"She jumped," Sheila replied. "For as strongly as she felt about the vow 'Till death do us part,' I'm surprised she didn't jump a long time ago."

"She wouldn't have jumped," Bob shouted. "I shouldn't have lied for you. I'm going to tell the police my real alibi. You don't have an alibi, do you?"

"You won't breathe a word. You're just as spineless as your astroturf. You thought my parents would hand you her job, didn't you? But you were wrong. So, so wrong, Bob. I'm your boss now."

"What? You got the promotion? When?"

"Who's got the last laugh now, corn-curl boy?" Sheila's voice dripped with scorn.

I tiptoed closer, trying to hear more clearly through the bat head. A wing creaked, and I froze, but they were yelling.

"That's it, we're finished!" Bob roared.

A slam made me jump—a chair thrown to the floor?—and my wings slapped audibly against the cement wall. I cringed. Couldn't they hear me? But they kept yelling.

"We were never anything, anyway. Who will they believe? You, her abusive husband, or me, her loving twin sister?" Sheila shouted.

I heard another sound, a loud metal banging this time. The vibrations echoed down the hallway. I flinched and heaved myself into the women's executive bathroom, bat suit creaking and slapping against walls, then cracked the door so I could hear and peek through. I slid down the wall, wrapping my wings in tight.

"Shit, woman! You swung a bat at me? You are so lucky you missed. You could've killed me."

Fast, heavy footsteps ran past me. It was Bob, blaring now towards the stairwell by the elevator.

I caught a glimpse of Sheila running after him, a silver metal bat in her hand.

Sheila hollered into the stairwell. "If I pushed Denise, she deserved it! I've been second to her since we were born, and I'm not going to be second to anyone anymore! Not even you!"

Oh my God. A confession.

I heard Bob's voice, muffled now. "You pushed her? You crazy-weirdo lunatic! Are you out of your mind?"

Sheila was screaming now, at the top of the stairs. "If you think you're going to the police, maybe you need a push too!"

I stuck my bat-head out of the bathroom door—a split-second of Sheila swinging like a cocky homerun hitter, the metal bat flashing in the fluorescent lights.

As she strutted back to her office, pounding her heels into the cement floor, I quickly closed the door.

I couldn't believe it. Sheila killed Denise! At the restaurant, she had told me that Bob and her had been working together the evening her sister supposedly committed suicide. She had said, rather flippantly, that Denise was a pushover! She sounded grief-stricken in her car that day, but she'd meant pushover literally. If I didn't still have bat wings on, I could've slapped myself.

I had to get myself out of the stupid suit and call Russell! I had to get out of here before bat-swinging, stairs-pushing Sheila knew I was here!

I half-waddled, half-ran for the stairs in my big feet, but I didn't see Bob. I had to be painfully deliberate, even moving fast, or I knew I'd end up rolling down the steps. When I finally exited on the ground level, I heard the elevator door ding open. Sheila.

Bam. The door from the stairwell slammed shut behind me. Crap. She'd hear that.

Her head whipped around, but only halfway. I froze, leaning against the stairwell door, but it was locked from the outside. By some miracle Sheila marched down the ramp toward the locker room, away from me, and I heaved my heavy-costumed body up the ramp and dropped into the player's dugout.

Crouching down in the dugout's far corner, as far out of sight as possible, I tried with all my might to remove the bat head so I could pull the costume off my body. I'd been sweating, and now the thing was cemented to my skin like a wetsuit under water.

It was stuck.

I really hoped Bob was on his way to the police right now. Who was I kidding, though? Maybe he was headed home to eat himself into a corn curl stupor.

All at once, I heard the clicking of Sheila's heels echoing on the concrete next to the dugout. Click, click, click. If she came in here, she would question me for sure. I was in trouble. I needed help.

I picked up my phone, intent on texting Russell. Why had he been pulling so many double shifts? Why hadn't I told him about my new job this week? If I made it through tonight, I promised myself, I would never hide anything again. I texted a picture taken on the day of tryouts in the locker room—me trying to get the bat suit on over gym pants. No, that wasn't enough. My shaking fingers pressed the speaker and Russell's number.

The phone rang several times and went to voicemail.

I whispered as loudly as I dared through the neck hole toward the phone.

"I love you, Sheila killed Denise."

Not exactly the way to tell someone you love them with the word kill in the same sentence, but he needed to hear both messages in case I didn't survive. Even though my voice was muffled through the costume head, Sheila heard me.

"Batgirl," Sheila called out in a snarling voice. "I can hear you. Where are you?"

She charged into the dugout swinging the bat, her face streaked with rage.

I fled into the open field as lightning flashed in the sky.

"Ahhh!" Out in the open with nothing to shield me, I was a sitting duck—or technically, a running bat. Sheila raced after me. A large bat chased by a baseball bat-wielding, high fashion woman in stilettos. I ran.

After I rounded first base, I continued toward second, stopping long enough to step on my big bird feet, and yank them off with all my might.

"Get back here! Who do you think you are?" Sheila was right behind me, panting and hollering—Then I heard her fall with a screech. Her high-priced heels were probably toast. Note to self: Never wear heels to run the bases.

Sheila shoes came wizzing at my back. She's thrown them at me! Faster barefoot, she gained ground. I felt the bat slice into my right wing. In seconds, she would have me.

I turned and dodged to my right. I held both wings in my hands, spreading them out like I was flying, dodging in serpentine moves along the third base line, but she struck again knocking the left wing completely off. That's when somehow the mascot head loosened.

I ripped it off and turned to face Sheila. Luckily, the head made a great shield to thwart the thrashing chops of her bat. It was made of some kind of hard resin and barely dented beneath her swings. In a few minutes, however, the left side of the face flew completely off, causing both of us to stop and stare at its trajectory.

Then she rushed at me. As we wrestled on the mound, her arm became hooked on my other wing. She was out of breath and slowing down.

Suddenly, in a flash, the stadium floodlights blared on and a police officer came rushing from the ramp near the dugout.

"Stop! Put the bat down immediately," he shouted. "Freeze! Right where you are!"

I heard Sheila gasp, and I wiggled free of her grip, scrambling to run. I didn't know if the officer meant me—the "bat"—or the dented metal she was using as a weapon.

Incredibly, she didn't stop. Her wild swings made her run like an out-of-control windmill blade. I zigged and zagged, left, then right, then took a roll on the ground—sharp toward her left flank. She windmilled double-time, then up and down, and it seemed to drain her momentum. With a burst of adrenaline and bravery, I turned around and faced her, rushing at her with the remains of the broken bat head. I banged straight into her like a battering ram. One of the bat's pointed ears contacted her nose with a crunch.

The bat flew from her hand and she fell to the ground, screaming, "You animal! You've broken my nose!"

As she lay curled in a fetal position with her hands over her face, I picked up the bat and stood over her. In quick, deft motions, the police surrounded, handcuffed, and arrested her.

I was bending over, coughing like crazy, trying to catch my breath. An officer helped me stand up.

"Sergeant McCormick got your call. That was quick thinking. Good work."

"Thank you," I wheezed.

He gave me a little smile—half-grimace. "You okay?"

"Yeah," I coughed. "Just give me a minute." I limped toward the third baseline bleacher seats, my remaining bat wing dragging across the field.

Russell rushed out onto the field. "Mel, what's going on? Wait, why are you dressed like a bat?" He wiped the dirt from my face and lips. "Well, half-dressed."

My T-shirt had been pulled and yanked in my fight with Sheila, and it looked like over-sized pajamas on me now. My eyes welled up.

"Oh, Russell, I'm so sorry I didn't tell you. I came to the stadium the other day for a job. I'm the team mascot." I look down at the ruined costume. "I was the team mascot."

He pulled me into his arms.

"It's okay, Clutch. I'm really glad you're okay. I told you to be careful, remember?"

"I know. You did." I looked at Sheila Battle across the field in handcuffs. "Russell, I heard Sheila confess to killing her sister to Bob Morris. I knew something wasn't right about Denise's death. Sheila and Bob Morris were having an affair—he was sleeping with his wife's twin. Actually, she had her own little love triangle going with him and Rodriguez."

"Melody, I told you trouble finds you."

I squeezed him tighter, tears stinging my eyes. He leaned towards me and kissed me.

"Wait," I whispered. I took his hand and led him under the bleachers, out of sight of from the other officers. "I have always wanted to kiss a guy under the bleachers."

"Melody, tell Alex and J.J. I need to see you all in my office."

"Sure thing, Mr. Snugg."

I headed downstairs to find Alex and J.J., my arms filled with promotional T-shirts and hoodies.

"Gifts from you?" Alex asked.

"Yes, you guys can have them. I love baseball and the 'Bats,' but my days of being a mascot are done." I dropped the pile of stuff into his arms, half of it falling on the floor with a crinkling sound of half-dozen cellophane-covered T-shirts.

J.J. leaned over to help me pick them up, his eyes widening at all the swag. "Mel, how 'bout you join us for lunch?"

I'd uncovered a serious criminal and had gotten chased in a bat suit by a woman in stilettos trying to kill me, but it was back to business at Old Peaceful. Still, I deserved a lunch break.

"Race you across the parking lot," I answered. "Losers buy."

The two men moved around to the back of the van, and I was left alone with the body. I pushed the stretcher trying to get it over the lip of the doorframe, but it started to roll away...

Dial a Murderer

I'm Melody Shore, a twenty-eight-year-old career girl. A snapshot of my day might make you think I'm a secretary in the seventies with an awesome fashion sense, but I'm really a great vintage shopper and an astounding funeral assistant. I work at The Peaceful Rest and meet all types of people. Some helpful, some need help, some living, some dead, some call every day…

"I didn't answer your first two calls, Mom, because I was unwrapping today's floral deliveries so the flowers can breathe." I exhaled loudly.

"Melody, are you feeling okay? I can bring soup?" I could hear the pots in my mom's kitchen clanking as she pulled them from her cupboard.

"No, Mom. I'm alive and well. I'm working and I need a little space like I told you."

"We can discuss that when I call later, but I need a decision now about making the voter calls for the Pleasantview 'Make Your Vote Count' Committee," she said.

"You enjoy calling people, Mom. Why aren't you doing it?" I asked.

"Well, dear, the calls need to be made today. I don't have time. I've already scheduled myself to thin out my garden. My flowers are being suffocated by the weeds. Besides, you need to be more active in our community."

Suddenly irritated, I jumped out of my chair. My office was so tiny, I needed to walk around. I walked to the bathroom and stood in front of the mirror.

"Mom, I can't see how weeding takes precedence over helping Marsha, your best friend, and President of the voting committee."

"Melody, when I make a schedule, I don't want to change it. Remember the time I changed my plans and went shopping on Tuesday instead of Wednesday. That Shop Right manager should have been thankful that I didn't call the news. The way he talked as if he didn't have to honor my coupons."

She rambled on as I looked in the mirror and realized I should be thankful that the gene pool splashed in my favor. When she took a breath, I tried to change the subject.

"Mom, have you ever noticed how much I resemble Dad? I have his curly brown hair, green eyes, and long legs."

"Yes, and you get your fashion sense from me. Now that you mention it, I think we need a girl's shopping day. I'm available this Friday, Saturday, and Sunday. It could be a three-day event. We can even drive to Pittsburgh. I'll look at hotels…"

I sighed as I put the phone down. She was so loud I didn't need to put it on speaker so I could adjust my hair and makeup. As I smoothed out my floral red tiered ruffle skirt and reapplied my orchid unicorn lipstick, my mother continued on. I let her ramble. Maybe I got my tough attitude from my mother? The difference was her attitude tended to be negative and mine positive.

I applied some powder from my vintage compact. Daily calls and long voice messages from my mom hadn't troubled me when I lived eighty miles away in Pittsburgh. I used to spend my free nights at one of the many downtown restaurants or clubs, with coworkers, or on dates. But since March I'd been back home working as a funeral home assistant at The Peaceful Rest. Between the wakes for the elderly, and lunches with my mom's best friend, Marsha, my late twenties were starting to look like middle age. I looked closer in the mirror and put my compact away. Did my eyes look puffy?

Finally, when Mom's tirade circled back to how I spend too much time with her best friend and needed more friends my own age, I had to interrupt. "I have all the friends I need, thank you, Mom. And, as far as Marsha, we normally only talk for a few minutes. I do takeout and eat alone in my office. She is busy and the café is usually crowded."

"I'm only trying to be helpful, honey. You shouldn't be trapped in that office all the time alone. The book I got you should help. I put it in your purse. Oh, and I crocheted a cat bookmark for the best chapter."

I opened my purse, and sure enough, there it was. "Get Me Out of Here: A Slow and Steady Guide to Overcoming Claustrophobia," I read aloud. It had a picture of a panicked-looking turtle. "Why did you give me this?"

"It has some good pointers. Breathe in and out slowly. Stay calm. Count to ten and time your breaths," my mother answered excitedly.

A loud buzzer rang out. I ran back to my desk to see, in the security feed, a tall, middle-aged man in a suit at the service entrance. Parked next to the door was a white van with the words "HVCU" on it. It's the Homicide and Violent Crime's Unit van. They are the big guys from Stewart County. Pleasantview only has a six-person police force. I've seen Stewart County at our police station before, but never here at the funeral home. My boss, funeral director, Arthur Snugg usually picks up a body or hires removers to deliver the deceased. Today, however, he was out.

"I'm coming down!" I shouted into the intercom. Then I see Snugg walk across the parking lot and shake the guy's hand.

"What's happening, Melody?" My mother was still on the phone. She didn't disconnect.

"A body just arrived, and Mr. Snugg is here."

"What is he doing?" my mother demanded impatiently.

"Working, Mom."

"I just saw him at Marsha's with Meg Stevens. Is she there too?"

My mother knew everyone's business. She was right though. When I looked back at the screen, a beautiful woman walked up beside Snugg and rested her hand on his backside. Some things should be left unseen.

I couldn't hear what anyone was saying, but it seemed confidential because he gently steered her back to his Buick.

I recognized the woman from a viewing last week. What was this, widow number six?

"Melody, what are they saying?"

"They're just talking, Mom."

"About what?" she asked.

"I don't know. Maybe makeup tips." I laughed a little too hard. "He is a mortician. Although his makeup is more for 'ever after' and not for 'every day.'"

"Melody!"

I shocked my mom. Surprising. "Listen, Mom, I gotta go. You can't make the dead wait."

Arthur Snugg pulled a stretcher from the HVCU van and was pushing it toward the door. I picked up a monogrammed "PR" pen and notepad and took the stairs to the lower-level past Alex and J.J.'s office, the floral room, casket storage, and cosmetic room to meet them. I was about to head to the embalming room—I called it the holding tank—when I realized a detective's presence meant it was another victim of some crime. Maybe even a murder.

I stopped and turned back to the stairs. The heel of my 1960s slingbacks hovered above the bottom step and I braced myself on the brass handrail. I was starting to wonder if I attracted trouble. I'd uncovered two murders already in the short time since I returned to Pleasantview. But I couldn't sit this one out. The mystery was too much.

I pushed open the door and it collided with the front of the stretcher.

"Oops, Mr. Snugg, I was coming to help. I hope I didn't hurt anything?" I started to straighten the edges of the body bag.

"I doubt it. She's pretty chill." The guy from Stewart County gave a small laugh as he continued to write on his clipboard. His tie hung loose, and his non-tailored three-piece suit was early eighties. He wasn't clean-shaven and he was sweating.

"Well, it might be a good day to be on ice," I said, as I fanned myself with my notepad. It was already heating up to be a warm June day. I glanced up at the outside wall thermometer. It read seventy degrees and it was only a little after ten a.m.

"Detective Roberts," the man said, holding out his hand.

"This is my new assistant, Melody Shore." Snugg introduced us with a quick nod. I shook his hand and turned to Snugg.

"I see we have a new arrival." I readied my tablet and pen. "When the family comes in to make arrangements do you think the Rose Room or Lilac Room will be better?"

"It will probably be best to…"

Detective Roberts loudly cleared his throat, turned to Snugg, and said, "Arthur, can we speak privately for a moment?" He motioned toward his van.

"Melody, please take the deceased into the funeral home." Arthur

Snugg pushed the stretcher toward me.

The two men moved around to the back of the van, and I was left alone with the body. I pushed the stretcher trying to get it over the lip of the doorframe, but it started to roll away. Before I could catch it, the stretcher nearly collided with the van's side.

"The wheels must be malfunctioning," I said loudly. Neither the detective nor Snugg looked up. Their heads were close together in discussion. I knelt, pretending to adjust the wheels anyway. The near accident worked to my advantage. I could overhear the detective whispering to Snugg.

"Arthur, this is a highly confidential matter. Please refrain from disclosing her identity to anyone in the town…"

I couldn't hear the rest of what Detective Roberts said over Snugg's car alarm. Meg Stevens must have set it off.

"Artie, I was reaching for my purse," she hollered from the Buick.

Arthur Snugg walked back over to me as the detective returned to his forms.

"So will the family be calling or stopping in?" I asked Snugg.

"What's that? No, I misspoke. The deceased is Ana Morrez. I will handle everything regarding Ms. Morrez. Direct any calls, inquiries, requests regarding her to me only."

"What's wrong? I mean, I can handle it."

"No, this is a police issue. For security reasons, I don't want you working on this one, Melody. I appreciate it, but it's not possible in this case. Now, let's put Ms. Morrez in morgue 2A. I will padlock it and let the boys know tomorrow when they return from their class that no one should disturb the body."

"Sure thing, Boss. You got it!" I tried not to look disappointed that he was now pushing the stretcher.

I followed him and the detective inside. When they took the body into the "holding tank," I headed back up the stairs to my office. Arthur Snugg didn't pay me enough for that.

Upstairs, I looked out the side draped lobby window. Snugg stood back outside and the plain white box van with the logo HVCU was hightailing it out of the funeral home parking lot. That detective was out for the speedy award for killed and chilled. Or, maybe, he couldn't get away quick enough from the PDA taking place between the reunited lovebirds in the parking lot.

I was back at my desk when Snugg and Meg Stevens came inside. I pulled out some invoices to look busy.

"Melody," Snugg sang out. "Ms. Stevens and I have an appointment this morning. We will be in my office." He gently guided her away from the 'Life after Loss' brochures. "You remember Meg. She owns the Stevens Churchill Horse Farm outside of town."

"Yes, hello, Ms. Stevens." I held out my hand, but she pretended not to see it. By the look of her perfectly manicured nails, salon-styled hair and makeup, Louis Vuitton handbag, and matching white silk pantsuit, I'd bet that she doesn't do any of the day-to-day horse care or farming.

"We're discussing her profit-loss margin." Snugg adjusted his tie. "I minored in business and economics, and Meg wants me to share some tips and expertise. A healthy bottom line is important, so no interruptions please, Melody."

"Sure thing, Mr. Snugg." I gave my best smile.

"Meg, go relax upstairs in my office," Snugg said, as he pushed her toward the grand mahogany staircase. "I will be right up."

Meg Stevens' manicured fingers pulled on Arthur Snugg's sleeve. "Oh, Artie, I can't wait to see the grandfather clock you've been talking about. It's absolutely thrilling that it came from Germany, and you have the builder's design papers."

Arthur Snugg proudly announced, "It's a one-of-a-kind, original. Once the guts are removed, I can be buried in it."

Meg Stevens said nothing. What do you say after that comment? She strode up the steps calmly as a kaleidoscope of stained glass poured in on her white suit.

"Mr. Snugg." I tried to get his attention as he stared after her. "Since you are busy, I can handle her intake paperwork."

"Yes, wonderful, Melody," Arthur Snugg murmured, his eyes glued on his now-closed office door. He stroked his new goatee and combed his fingers through his graying temples. No doubt about it. He was in love again.

"What's wonderful, Mr. Snugg?"

"I mean, no. What I meant to say is this is a private police matter. Nothing about her being here should be disclosed."

"Got it. And you told the twins?" I looked at the security camera video next to my desk where I could usually see the boys—I mean, Alex and J.J—playing foosball in their office. They were Arthur Snugg's nephews through marriage.

"I'll tell them." He paused and looked out the window. "Somehow, when my ex-wife got an allowance in the decree for her nephews to work here until they turned thirty or passed the mortuary science program, I thought they would give up and go work at a gas station or something."

"I would like to know who her lawyer was."

Snugg cracked one of his rare smiles. "I think it was your old boss."

"So, they are actually taking a class?" I asked, closing the blank document I had opened to input her information.

"Yes. It's a funeral service management class. Perhaps some of these classes would interest you as well?" He looked at me. "Melody, I lost a lot more than a wife in the divorce. The Peaceful Rest has been in chaos without her. With your help, things have finally begun to get back to order."

"That's nice of you to say, Mr. Snugg. And don't worry, anything, anything at all regarding Ana Morrez—calls, inquiries, requests, they are all yours."

"Thank you, Melody." He looked at his watch and glided up the staircase like an ice skater, or was it more like Count Dracula?

As he entered his office, I heard his grandfather clock chime. The perfect entrance. Could he possibly think that his weird hourly chiming clock would turn women on? Creepy. It's a six-foot, black walnut, early 1900's German grandfather clock with an eagle, wolf, and bear carved into the wood. He never stops talking about how much it cost and how rare it was. I thought it was kinda ugly, in that the wolf's eyes seemed to glow, and the bear's mouth was open, baring sharply carved teeth.

With Snugg and his newest love interest tucked away in his office, I decided it was lunchtime. I forwarded my desk phone, grabbed my purse, and hung the lunch sign on the door since Alex and J.J. weren't around. The sign read, "Morticians take Lunch too. Feel Free to Roam the Grounds. Be Back Before Eternity." The former Mrs. Snugg had an odd sense of humor.

I headed down Republic Street toward Main. As I walked down Main Street, I crossed over Fifth, and then turned and detoured slightly toward the flag-decorated building on Fifth belonging to my closest friend, Claire Cottage. I waved at her through the window, and she motioned for me to come inside, pointing to a pile of clothing she was sorting through. I could see a spaghetti strap, wide-legged, olive-colored jumpsuit hanging next to her sales counter. I considered stopping in for a second until my stomach growled and the smell of the grills cooking outside the Corner Cupboard caused me to shake my head and keep walking.

My phone buzzed and the screen lit up with Russell's handsome face. I never expected to come back home after the worst breakup ever, only to find the man of my dreams. I stared at the picture. Who could resist that stubble beard, that curly hair that begged for my fingers to run through it, and Irish whiskey brown eyes?

Russell was a sergeant for our local police department. Snugg never said I couldn't ask Russell about Ana Morrez. I mean, it was official police business, right?

"How goes it, Clutch?"

"Russell McCormick...you've been taking your duty to serve and protect pretty seriously. Not that I mind...I'm glad you called. I need to know. Do you know anything about Ana Morrez?"

"Ana Morrez?" Russell asked in his deep police officer voice.

"Yes, she's the deceased of the day. Snugg just told me he doesn't want me to handle her arrangements. I don't get it. I'm basically running Old Peaceful during his 'rebound' romances."

"Yeah, how could he? What a boss! Grrrr," Russell said.

"You don't have to mock me! It's Snugg, not me."

"I'm sorry, Mel. Instead of a quick morning trip to Pleasant Creek, I had to come into work early. As far as Snugg, I'm sure he realizes what an asset you are, but he has to work with the police on this one." Russell sighed.

"Oh, good. So, you know everything. Spill."

"I'm hoping it's me you're interested in going out with, and not just to grill me for information about Ana Morrez." Russell chuckled softly.

"Nope. Ha ha, kidding. I care about you, babe."

"Seriously, leave this one alone, Melody. Let the tough guys handle it."

"I'm going to pretend you didn't say that. I'm tough." Staying out of it wasn't going to be easy because Ana Morrez was actually here, one floor below me, and everyone seemed to know who she was but me.

"Melody, what about tonight?" he asked, changing the subject.

"Remember how I volunteer at the animal shelter?"

"Yep."

"I kind of told them you were coming to help out tonight. We are short-handed. We gotta prepare cages for six new cats."

"What do we have to do?"

"Well, we'll make forever friend bags, and prepare paperwork for the adoption fair which is tomorrow."

"Another day and evening spent wishing I was fishing. Hey, maybe tonight I can get a cat. They like fish."

"I'm pretty sure cats like their fish in a can…" I said. "But seriously, I would adopt one if my landlord, John, would allow pets in my apartment."

"That's exactly what you need, an animal cuter than me vying for your attention." Russell laughed.

"Let's meet a little after five. It's the Furry Friends Animal Shelter on Route fifty," I said.

"I'll pick you up!"

"That's sweet of you," I countered. "But I drove Blue Betty here. I can at least drive myself."

"I know you can, but who was there for you when Blue Betty had a flat tire last week?"

"I just like to watch your muscles flex under your T-shirt. If you weren't so cute, I would have called roadside assistance."

At Marsha's Café, there wasn't a single seat at the counter, and the six booths that lined the white-painted brick walled café were either filled or needed to be bussed. Three people stood ahead of me in line, staring hungrily at their two-page menu as they waited for one of the unoccupied booths. I placed my order of Harvest Turkey wrap, homemade chips, and freshly brewed ice tea and went to sit at a large wooden picnic table outside the storefront in the June sunshine.

"I saw you place your order, so I thought I would bring it out myself, Melody." Marsha placed the food down in front of me and then squeezed her large frame into the bench seat. She smelled like vanilla and her dyed-blond hair was lighter from both highlights and baking flour.

"Hi, Marsha! This looks delicious. Thank you."

"Sure thing. How are you, Melody?" She put her arm around my shoulder.

"Everything's going good." I bit into my wrap, and homemade mayo dripped down my chin. Marsha handed me a napkin.

"The funeral home and Arthur Snugg treating you okay?"

"It's great—" I took a drink of my ice tea. "My mom called this morning. She said you needed help to make calls for some special election committee?"

"Oh, Melody, your mom doesn't realize how busy you are. But I'm always glad to have you around."

"Honestly, I would like to help make the calls, if I can."

"It is an emergency vote to fill an empty seat in our town council."

"Why is there an open seat?"

"Ana Morrez. She was head of the council. She passed away last night."

"Ana Morrez?" I took another bite of my turkey wrap to cover my shocked face. "Do you know what happened to her? Why can't this wait 'til the next election?"

"We have a vote on the animal shelter funding next week. Without the votes, we could lose the no-kill status we worked so hard to get." Marsha sighed.

"What will happen if we don't get someone on the council in time?"

"Without a pro-animal rights voice on the council, the shelter will turn back into a pound again. It's cheaper for the township. Animals get thirty days, then they euthanize them."

"What, no! How cruel!" I teared up.

"Don't cry, Melody. Can I bring you some cake?"

"Oh, Marsha, thanks, but lunch was good. Do you know what happened to Ana Morrez?"

"It's so sad." Marsha's eyes filled. "She doesn't have any local family. They found her at a hotel twenty miles east. We don't even know if they will be bringing her body back to bury," Marsha said, dabbing her eyes with a napkin. "And it's going to be tough to fill her shoes. She was the reason we now have a no-kill shelter. She was great—she also pushed for a lot of road and park improvements and got our town a lot of funding."

As much as I liked Marsha, I couldn't say anything until I found out exactly what happened to her and what all the secrecy was about.

"Melody, are you okay? You look a little pale."

"Yeah, Marsha, I'm fine. I volunteer there and I really love animals. We can't lose the shelter."

"Well, Charles Williams is here eating lunch. He is a big proponent of the shelter. When you're done, I'll introduce you. I'm sure he would like to meet a volunteer." She squeezed me one more time and I inhaled her sugar cookie scent. "That would be great. I'm sure I can make these calls. For sure!"

"Okay, let me get you the list of some of the phone numbers we want to call." Marsha hurried back into the café and returned a few minutes later. "These people are supporters of the shelter. I divided up the calls, so you only have to make about twenty." She handed me a sheet of phone numbers. On top was a page of information about the Pleasantview Township Council.

"So, Steve Callow, Elaine Munsing, and Charles Williams. Two men, one woman." I read the names. "These are the people running for Ana's seat?"

"Yes, the other four board members still have two years left in their terms. So, Steve, Elaine, or Charles will be voted in as the fifth member. We have always had five in case of a tie vote." Marsha walked to a nearby table, wiped it clean, and returned to me.

"Okay, let's see here. Three people running, Steve Callow, Elaine Munsing, and Charles Williams. This will be easy and won't take long. I'll make these calls." I tucked the list into my bag.

"That would be super. Hold on, I have something else," Marsha said. "For you and your boyfriend to enjoy tonight." She handed me a white bakery box.

"Oh, thank you. You are so sweet!" I peered in. Half a chocolate cake with fluffy white icing. "I already said I'd make the calls, Marsha! I'm sure Mr. Snugg won't mind me doing my civic duty."

I had just finished my lunch when screams erupted from the café. A middle-aged man and a tall, gray-haired woman with severely cut bangs burst through the doors in a heated argument. The man removed his baseball cap that read "Big Business is my Business" and shouted, "Elaine, you couldn't read a budget if it reached up and bit your fat ass. We needed to make budget cuts yesterday."

"I'll show you cuts," screamed the woman, her eyes wild, wielding a butter knife. She jabbed at the angry man, her long red nails dangerously near his eyes.

They were both followed by a waitress with black hair, and soon a concerned crowd filtered out of the restaurant onto the patio.

Elaine turned to the server. "Are you prying into our private conversation?" She threw the knife down on the ground and drove off in a yellow BMW.

About four feet away from my table, a man in large wire-rim glasses joined Mr. Big Business. "It was such a dreadful shame about Ana," he said with a British accent. "But I believe I was quite proper in bringing up the park funding before we vote on Tuesday."

"Teaming with Elaine will get you nowhere," Big Business answered. "You lost last time. You'll lose again."

"The vote will determine who wins!" Marsha said. "The people want change and improvements! You are causing a scene here. If you don't leave, I am going to call the police."

Both men stormed off in different directions.

"What happened? Are you all right, Deena?" Marsha said to the server who'd been threatened. Deena began to cry.

"It's not your fault." Marsha patted Deena on the shoulder. "I mean, you are employee of the month. I can't imagine you gave her poor service...I mean, not enough to scream at you."

"I was trying to listen in. I mean, the whole town is talking about Ana," Deena said.

"Who was that woman with the knife?" I asked.

"That was Elaine Munsing." Deena sniffed.

"Should we report her? She seems unhinged. Is she dangerous, I mean?"

"Melody, no. We can't do that, hon." Marsha cleared the tables while Deena sat helplessly sniffling into a lace handkerchief. Weird music played a little too loudly without the lunch crowd.

"Whoa, wait…" I stared at Marsha. "That woman that stormed out of here—she's the same woman on the top of the voter sheet you gave me! Elaine Munsing. She's a candidate, isn't she?"

"Might as well scratch her. Who's going to vote for her? Especially now, right?" Marsha said.

"Deena, what was Elaine saying when you were waiting on her table, that you could overhear?" I gently asked.

"It didn't make sense—any of it. I overheard her say, 'You should have dug the holes first,' and, 'How much money did you get?'"

"What do you think she was referring to?" I stood and picked up the cake Marsha had given me.

"I wish I knew. She is a horrible woman." Deena grabbed an armful of dishes to take inside. "Remember when Elaine got in a fight with Ana Morrez?"

"I guess she's not sad that Ana is gone?" I followed Marsha and Deena back into the café.

"Sad but probably true, Melody," Marsha said.

"What about the other candidates? Were they friends?" I asked.

"Well, Charles Williams lost to Ana by a two percent margin last time," Marsha answered. "Ana was pro parks and animals like Charles and Elaine claim to be."

"What about Steve Callow? You didn't mention him," I said, looking at the sheet Marsha had given me earlier.

"Steve Callow is all about cutting recreational funding and bringing big business to Pleasantview."

"Have you ever seen anything violent before like this knife fight, we witnessed?" I asked Marsha.

"You know, at the May meeting, I saw Charles and Ana in a heated discussion next to Ana's car. I heard him say, 'You don't know what I am capable of.' Then he stormed off."

My floral bangle watch read two forty-five p.m. After the screaming
match at Marsha's, I didn't want to make the phone calls, but I promised
I would. I sat spinning a half-circle back and forth in my office chair (I
would have spun a full circle, but the size of my office didn't allow it), then
I got up and peered out into the foyer, looking up the staircase towards
Arthur Snugg's office. As if on cue, Snugg's door opened. He and Meg
emerged and stood at the top of the staircase, laughing and whispering.
No, that's not awkward that her silk suit coat was all wrinkled! Down the
staircase came the new couple.

"Meg, you go on to the car. Here are the keys." She took them from his
hand, lingering a little too long.

"Melody, I need to go out for a while. Do you have everything under
control?"

"All's well." I gave him two thumbs up.

"Okay. If I'm not back today, make sure to set the alarms and lock up."

I refrained from saying that it was my job every night. Instead, I nodded. Arthur Snugg walked to the door, but then he turned back as we both
heard a love song playing from his office.

"I forgot to shut off my radio." He moved toward the staircase to his
office.

"I'll get it, Mr. Snugg."

"Melody, I almost forgot the call you put through to me yesterday
morning, Mr. Williams wants to stop by later regarding arrangements.
Standard requests and needs. I know you have wanted to get into this part
of the business, so I'm giving you this one. You don't mind handling this,
right? It's at four thirty. Thanks, Melody. Meg, Meg, I'm coming."

He hurried out the door. I walked to the window and pulled back the
bunched-up cream curtain as his Buick drove across the blacktop parking
lot and out onto Republic Street.

Wait! What'd he say? He wanted me to handle an appointment? I wonder if I will get a commission. I did a happy dance, and my ruffle skirt
shook and spun. This was my chance to show him I could handle the
position of Assistant Funeral Director.

Arthur Snugg kept his office extremely clean. A large, dark cherry desk with an enormous leather chair sat on one side of the room. Two antique tapestry chairs were in front of his desk to give the client's families a place to sit. His office was framed on two sides by windows and two panel walls. Against one wall sat an overstuffed leather couch with velvet brown throw pillows, normally stacked neatly in one corner. On the other paneled wall was his prized clock, and a door that looked like a closet door but had hidden steps allowing easy access to the lower level without going back into the main reception area. I imagined when he wasn't in here talking on the phone to his latest love or romancing them amongst the throw pillows on the couch, he spent his free time polishing the clock.

I shut the radio off, trying not to gag at "Love Me Tender" blaring from it, and the throw pillows not neatly stacked anymore—and that's when I saw the "Morrez" file laying right in the middle of his desk.

Technically, I wasn't lying to Snugg. I certainly would let him handle everything. But part of my job was to make sure all the paperwork was complete and the filing of her death certificate and insurance policies was timely. He would thank me for taking the initiative. One of his favorite things to say was, "preparation is key." Of course, usually, he meant the bodies in the holding tank. As a funeral director, he did things I didn't like to think of…although I was pretty sure his motto applied to the office, too. I mean, to do my job and prepare everything he needed, I had to look at her file, right?

"Right," I said aloud. My fingers drummed on the file and with one quick flip of the plain tan manila folder cover, Ana Morrez's file opened.

I quickly glanced over it. The death certificate listed her name, Ana A. Morrez, age fifty-two, and cause of death was a single gunshot wound. Mr. Snugg, the Stewart County guy, and even Russell must have been keeping this quiet as it was an ongoing investigation. Did they suspect the killer was here in Pleasantview?

When I returned to my desk, I pressed the message button on my desk phone console. Two messages. I played the first one.

"Hey Melody, Alex and J.J. here. We tried Uncle Arthur and can't get him. Are you avoiding us too?"

I was about to phone them back to ask if their funeral service management class had kicked them out when a delivery man walked in.

"Got a delivery here for Mr. Arthur Snugg."

"He's not available, but I'm Melody Shore. You can bring the package in and I'll sign."

"Um." He squinted in the dim light. "In here?"

"Sure, I'll carry it up to his office."

He looked up the large staircase.

"You? It's two caskets. I was thinking more of using my dolly or an elevator depending on where I am going with them."

"Oh, okay, I didn't realize. In that case, meet me around back."

"If you could check them out and sign here," the delivery guy said after he unloaded the caskets.

"Sure, good idea. I need to make sure they arrived in A+ shape. Can I get a copy of that, so I can enter the invoice?" I struggled to remove the wrap that covered one. "Boy, they wrap them good."

"Here, I got it." He pulled out a box cutter and expertly sliced through the covering, revealing a shiny bronze casket. As he continued the second one, I opened the first casket, pulled the plastic packing rim off the lip, and peered in. A brochure lay on top of the pristine cream liner.

"This is interesting." I read the brochure to him. "Says here, these state-of-the-art caskets with auto-locking lids eliminate the need to seal the caskets. They are a strong selling point with families...I can see the commercial now. I've risen from the dead, but I can't get out..."

"Ha ha," he said. "Hey, I got one," he continued, unwrapping the second one. "Someone called and tried to sell me a casket the other day...I said that's the last thing I need."

We both stood there laughing at our warped senses of humor. I added another one. "Do you think glass coffins will ever be popular?"

"Remains to be seen," we both said at once.

I had been spending too much time with Alex and J.J.

After the delivery guy left, I spent the rest of the afternoon typing and filing the invoicing and insurance paperwork, but I couldn't stop thinking about what happened at the café. What happened to Ana Morrez? Why would no one release her information to the town?

Things didn't add up. I made a list:

What I don't know & What I'd Like to Know:

Why such secrecy around Ana Morrez?

What did Russell know about her?

Why would they bring her body here to Pleasantview?

Why tell Arthur Snugg and not tell anyone else?

Snugg's grandfather clock chimed from above. I'd completed my "to do" pile, and my desktop was empty except for the papers Marsha gave me. The list of numbers to call for the election loomed in front of me. Better start the calls so I have time to gather papers for my meeting. First I had to practice: *Hi, I'm Melody Shore, calling to ask you to please come to the special election being held in Town Hall at six p.m. tomorrow to fill the vacant council seat of Ana Morrez. The community needs your voice and your vote. Our animals, parks, and libraries are counting on you.*

After two trial runs, I picked up the phone and dialed.

"Hi, I'm Melody Shore, calling to…"

"Whatever you're selling I'm not buying," said a man's voice.

"Um…."

Click.

I dialed the next one.

"Hi, I'm calling from The Peaceful Rest Funeral Home to ask you to a meeting to…"

"Is this one of those invitation calls where I come to your presentation, and you feed me dinner and try to sell me a funeral or something?" the man who answered asked.

"Huh? We don't offer dinner when you…"

Click.

"Hi, I'm Melody, calling to ask you to the special election at six p.m. tomorrow, Town Hall to elect Ana Morrez. Oh, shoot to replace Ana Morrez. Our parks, pooches, and books. Oh, man."

Click.

"Hi, I'm Melody from The Peaceful Rest Funeral Home, calling…"

"Since when do funeral homes make cold calls?" a man asked.

"Well, I am calling from a funeral home, but it's about…"

"Hey, honey, death's at the door. They're calling! And, it's for you." The man chuckled into the phone and hung up.

"I don't know who you are, but this call isn't funny," the next woman screamed into my ear.

Click.

I was about to dial another number when my phone rang.

"Hi Mom…nope, nothing new since this morning…yeah, I saw Marsha. I'm making the calls now. Bye, Mom."

Sheesh! I dialed the next number.

"Hi, I'm Melody, inviting you to a special election. Town Hall at six p.m. tomorrow to fill the council seat of Ana, Ana Morrez. Your voice and vote count. Our parks, animals, and libraries need you."

"I'll tell you what, honey, if you want to come over, we can talk about what we both need," a man said.

"What? How about this, I'm calling to invite you to a council meeting where you can make a difference with your vote, not with me, bud! Goodbye!" I hit the disconnect on my cell phone with such force that I broke one of my newly painted nails.

As I dialed my next call, the front doors of the funeral home flew open and Alex and J.J. walked in and paraded through the lobby. Loud music blared from the tiny speaker Alex was carrying. They were both dressed in Hawaiian shirts. Alex wore pale pink shorts. J.J.'s shorts were bright teal with pineapples.

"Hey, Mel!" J.J., a silly grin on his face, did his crazy legs dance steps outside my office.

"Turn that music off now! Geez, what are you wearing?" I shouted.

"What? Who is this? I will listen to classical music all day if I want. And, if I want to wear my pajamas all day, I will. I knew these new phones spied on you!"

"Oh, boy! Sorry, wrong number. Please ignore this call," I said.

Click.

"Uncle Arthur around?" J.J. picked up my phone list and papers and held them out of reach.

"No, he isn't. Why?"

"We need to borrow a few bucks," Alex said.

"How was the funeral services class?" I asked.

"We passed," J.J. answered and then yawned.

"Ha! I'd like to see proof. The only thing you two ever pass is the football to each other in the parking lot." I reached for my papers.

"We didn't technically pass yet. But I bet we will. They will send the scores in two days." Alex grabbed the papers away from J.J. and neatly arranged them back on my desk.

"Hey, Alex, doesn't Uncle A keep money up in that box we made him in eighth grade? What did he call it? His hopeless chest." He pushed past Alex, running up the staircase into Arthur Snugg's office. The clock chimed loudly.

"I'm not getting blamed for missing money," I hollered.

As I dialed the first six numbers of my next call–814-977–Alex and J.J. tiptoed by and ran out the front doors. J.J. was carrying a white bakery box. My cake!

"I saw what you did! I'll make you pay!" I screamed. My free hand slammed down on my desk. "And how much money did you take?"

That's when I realized someone had answered the call I had just dialed. At first, they said nothing, but I could hear deep breathing.

"Who is this? I will trace this call and find you."

"This is Melody Shore..."

Click.

I ran to the front door and flung it open. Alex and J.J. turned onto Republic Street. I was cakeless.

"This isn't a free cake funeral home!" I shouted out to the empty parking lot.

Back in my office, I threw the phone call list in the garbage and sighed. I'd just have to get another cake. I pulled from my desk drawer a packet that contained a plot map, price sheets for lots, standard burial versus cremation costs, and one of my newly printed business cards. It was four thirty. My appointment should arrive at any minute.

The grandfather clock upstairs chimed five times. It echoed down the stairs—the only noise in the funeral home besides me doing half-spins in my chair. Charles Williams was a no-show. Russell must be on his way to the animal shelter. Maybe I'd get there earlier.

"Leaving now, see you soon," I texted with a few heart emojis.

I put the packets I pulled back in my drawer and got up to set the alarms, turn off the main lighting and close the doors for the evening, when my phone console display caught my eye. The other message I'd forgotten to listen to after the delivery guy showed up.

I hit the play button.

"This is Charles Williams calling for Mr. Snugg. I will be slightly late this evening. I apologize. Bye for now."

He was coming and his voice sounded British. Could it be the guy from the café? Could he be the one Marsha was going to introduce me to? How many Charles Williams could there be in Pleasantview? I pulled the paperwork back out and arranged it on my desk. Now I would be late for meeting Russell.

My phone dinged.

"Wait there. I'm fifteen minutes away. I have a surprise for you," Russell texted back. He was coming here. I attempted to text back a kiss emoji, but my finger accidentally pressed the frightened emoji. I was about to send another when someone walked in. It was the guy that Elaine Munsing was arguing with today, Mr. Big Business, arrived, still wearing his cap, a weasely glint in his pale-yellow eyes.

"Um...how can I help you?"

"Tell me what you saw!" He pulled out a gun and aimed his skinny arms directly at me.

"Whoa, why is everyone involved in this election so violent?"

"What do you know about Ana Morrez?" He quizzed me.

"A...Ana, Ana Mor..Morrez?" I stuttered.

"Yes, you better tell me now," he demanded.

"Ana Morrez, the head of council? I'm making vvvvvolunteer vvvoting calls, reminding voters to come out and fill her position. I didn't personally know her, other than I know she was probably murdered...Oops!"

"You know she was murdered!" His high-pitched voice bellowed through the empty funeral home.

"Let's forget I said that. I'm going to ask you to please calm down. If you talk any louder, you'll wake the dead," I said in a weak attempt at bravery.

He pushed his hair out of his eyes and looked like he might actually shoot me.

"Please, put the gun down."

"If you don't tell me what you know and why you called me, I will do to you what I did to her," he said with a growl.

"Listen, I didn't call you. Wait? You did something to Ana Morrez?"

"I mean it. Spill what you know, or else." He took a step closer.

"What do you want me to talk about?" How many people were going to pull a gun on me at this job? I was getting annoyed. Where was Russell? How long ago was fifteen minutes? "I told you, I didn't personally know her. What did you do to her?" I couldn't imagine I had been sitting in the same café with this guy a few hours ago.

"This is your last chance. Why did you call and threaten me?" He cocked his gun.

The front doorbell chimed, and the doors plowed open. The older guy from the café with big wire-rim glasses walked in, removed his hat and jacket, and looked at us.

My adrenaline kicked in and I screamed, "You two work this out! I am out of here!"

I ran up the steps two at a time and into Arthur Snugg's office, closed the door, and locked it. Finally, I understood why Snugg wanted a little privacy. Did killers on the loose happen before I started working here? Because it seems like a thing now.

Wait…I was safe for a minute, but I had nowhere to go! I was trapped. A shot rang out. I ducked under Snugg's desk. Someone busted the locked door open, and a bullet shot into the priceless grandfather clock. Wood splintered and glass shattered like a "nail bomb," causing a hail of glass and toothpicks to rain down on his immaculate office. The mechanism and front face had sprung forward and struck the attacker knocking him off his feet. From my hiding spot under the desk I could see the bottom of his shoes. Maybe he was knocked out for good. I could see Snugg's closet door too. Then I remembered it had access to the lower level. A way out!

Suddenly brave, I shouted, "Arthur Snugg is going to make you pay for that clock. He was planning on being buried in it. Do you know what that does to a funeral director?" I pulled open the door to the lower level and escaped.

"You're the one who is going to pay!" he said in a snarl.

"Not today, Satan!" Faster than a point guard at the three-second clock, I ran down the steps to the lower level.

I stopped momentarily outside the embalming room door. I didn't know, nor did I want to know, what was in this room that I could use to protect myself. Where was Russell? I fumbled with my phone. I heard my intruder open the door, so I raced into the open door of the cosmetic room. Too late, I realized there was a body laid out on the table. Grabbing a can of hairspray, I crouched down between a tall cabinet and a tray of a set of Forever After makeup.

A few moments later, the shadow of a hand and a gun appeared on the wall, and he stepped into the middle of the room. I stood up and snuck up behind him.

"Hi-yah!" I brought my arms down with a karate chop on the back of his neck.

His gun went off, then slid under the table with the dead body on it.

"What the hell!" He went for the gun, but the body laid out in full hair and makeup made him back away. He turned back toward me. I sprayed him in the face with a dusting of hairspray that would hold hair in place through a category three tornado. I ran, but he shoved me backward and I fell against the light switch, causing the lights to turn on. He dropped down on his knees in search of his gun.

Thankfully, the cosmetic room was not as neat as Arthur Snugg's office. There on a table was an open container of glue, which Snugg used for things I didn't want to think about, and what appeared to be a small sewing needle. I grabbed the needle and with all the force I could muster, stabbed it down on my attacker's shoulder.

"Ow! You are going to pay for that," he shouted, turning his face upwards toward me.

I picked up the glue off the table and dumped it on his face. Some of it went into his eyes and mouth. He tried to rub it off, but the more he rubbed, the more he swore.

Jumping up off the floor, he ran to the sink and turned on the water, putting his head under the flow. I don't know what was in the stuff, but he screamed like I'd pepper-sprayed him, shouting obscenities and swinging his windmill-like arms.

"Oh my God, oh my God!" I had to escape. I ran to the casket room. Inside sat our full range of a dozen caskets from expensive to plain. Some were open, including the new auto-locking ones that the delivery guy had brought today.

My attacker staggered into the room. His eyes and mouth were swollen and red, barely able to open. Globs of glue chunked his face into a poorly made Halloween mask. I raced at him and knocked him over into the new locking model. Thinking quickly, I swung his legs up and in and slammed the lid, locking him in.

I heard a thud. Was Russell finally here? Or was it the British guy coming to finish me off?

Desperate for a place to hide until I was sure what the thud was, I climbed into the nearest casket and shut the lid.

It clicked.

What had I done? My heartbeat sounded like a deafening drum, but it wasn't as loud as my mind replaying the words from the brochure this afternoon, "These state-of-the-art caskets with auto-locking lids eliminate the need to seal the caskets. These are a strong selling point with families." Obviously, the click meant I had jumped into the upgrade.

"Oh Lord, oh Lord, what do I do now?" I prayed quietly; afraid my attacker would hear me.

I couldn't tell if he was in one of the locked caskets or had climbed out of his coffin, or even knew that I was still in the room. I lay silently, trying not to move. Although I don't think anyone could tell I was moving inside the small two-foot area I was confined in. I could wiggle my toes and bend my legs and lift my head to a ten-degree angle, but that was the extent of movement.

Rolling over was not an option. The click surely meant I was locked in. I had no backup plan. I was going to die. As I attempted to breathe through my nose and slowly out my mouth to calm myself, I felt myself hyperventilating.

Wait! What did Houdini do when trapped in a small space? How did he escape? He escaped because he knew how to slow his breathing and hold his breath under water. I might run out of air, but at least I didn't have to hold my breath.

Breathing. That reminded me of something. My last thoughts as I was about to black out were of the claustrophobia book my mom put in my purse this morning. Placing my hands over my heart, I think of what she said earlier. I breathe in and out slowly, count to ten, and timed my breaths, listening for any noise outside of my heartbeat which was still thundering in my ears.

It worked.

"Dear, Lord, please help me and watch over Russell if I don't make it out of this. Please make sure another woman is not an option too quickly. And please look down on Arthur Snugg when he returns in the a.m. to find me dead and his so-loved clock and funeral home in shambles."

As I lay there, my mind reeled with thoughts of my attacker. What brought him to the funeral home and why was he trying to kill me? I knew nothing about Ana Morrez, other than she was killed by a single gunshot wound, and I'd spent the afternoon making calls to find a replacement for her. Did Charles Williams have anything to do with this? He'd lost to her by a narrow margin last time, and I had been making calls for voters that supported his agenda. Perhaps he made the appointment to gain access to the funeral home to find something out. But what? The only thing I knew for sure was I didn't want to meet the other council members.

And why did the angry guy from the café come here? And why was he trying to kill me? He acted like I'd called him. I didn't call him. Or did I? There was so much going on. I might have mistakenly called him.

Holy heck, I brought Ana Morrez's killer here by calling. Where is Russell?

I was so cramped and hot. I wish I hadn't tried to make myself more professional with my new buttoned long-sleeve, yellow cotton sweater. As I unbuttoned it, my hand felt my cell phone in my sweater pocket. I had an idea!

Able to move my arms slightly, I pulled the phone out of my pocket and hoped that reception would work in a casket. I needed to confirm my suspicion that I'd called my attacker here. I hit redial. Shazam! I could hear a loud music ringtone in the room. I was right! I didn't know if I would make it out of here or who would win the election, and if they would help Furry Friends, but I knew that my phone call brought my attacker here.

The next thing I heard was a voice I recognized.

"Mel, Mel, where are you?"

I banged against the lid and rocked the casket by throwing my body against the sides.

"Hurry, Russell, I'm in here. Don't open any other caskets but the one I'm in. Please hurry!" I screamed.

There was a banging on my casket lid.

"It's okay, Mel, I'm here. I'm going to open the lock."

I felt the casket being jarred back and forth. Seconds later, light streamed in and the lid opened. For once I was happy with false advertising: The locks were not tamper-resistant. I sat up and Russell wrapped me in his arms and lifted me out of my almost sealed fate.

"Oh, Mel, please be okay. You're okay, right? You're not hurt, are you? I'm so glad to see you!"

"Not as glad as I am to see you," I said as tears cascaded down my cheeks.

Russell kissed them away.

"Where have you been? Fifteen minutes was an hour ago!" My clenched fists pounded on his bulletproof vest as my head collapsed into his unyielding shoulder.

"I got your text and was running late too. I wanted to go together."

"You stopped to drive me?"

"Sort of, but once I got here and saw Mr. Williams, I phoned for backup."

"You know Mr. Williams?"

"Yeah, he is running for council and, I'm really sorry, Mel. Please don't cry. You're okay now. Your backup is here. I didn't tell you about Ana Morrez because it is an active murder investigation."

Several other officers stood nearby, guns drawn.

Looking quickly around the room, I noticed the intruder was not there.

"My attacker, the killer. Russell, he must still be in that casket," I said, pointing to the closed casket across the room.

"You locked him in a casket too? Clutch, you never cease to impress me."

He gestured toward his officers, and they opened the casket and pulled my attacker out.

His hair stood straight up. He must have run his hands through it and the three pounds of hairspray I doused him with held it upward. His almost-swollen-shut eyes peered at me and glue chunks still dotted his face. Bright red hives covered the glue-free portions of his face and neck.

"He confessed to me that he hurt Ana Morrez," I said, in a shaken voice.

"Get me out of here. That interfering secretary and her arsenal of weapons. Jail will be safer."

"Wait, don't let him leave." My fingers hit redial, and a loud ringing came from his pocket.

"Answer it, Mr. Callow," Russell commanded.

"Mr. Callow? Steve Callow?" I gasped.

"I was so sick of Ana not agreeing with my ideas. She voted for funding for parks and animals all the time. We needed to make cuts. I can bring in business! I can do so much more for Pleasantview!" he screamed. "She had to go so I could run the board. I am going to do so much more."

"The only thing you're going to do is go to jail," I yelled back.

An officer cuffed Steve Callow's hands behind his back and took him away.

"I can't believe I made a simple phone call, and this guy shows up and tries to kill me."

"You called Steve Callow here, Mel?" Russell asked.

"Callow's number was on my 'Make Your Vote Count' list. There was so much going on. I was preparing for Mr. Williams to arrive, and I dialed Callow. Then J.J. stole my cake and I shouted out that I 'knew what he had done.' Callow must have thought I was talking to him."

"Mel, you are going to have to tell me that again, slowly," Russell said.

"I think perhaps I can help," said Charles Williams. He spoke from across the room, on a stretcher, and gave me a small wave.

"Ana had phoned me last week to talk. She and I had an argument out in the parking lot after the last council meeting which I regret."

"About what?" I asked him.

"Trees."

"Trees?"

"I offered to plant them myself to save the town money because we didn't get as big of a grant as I hoped," he continued. "Ana said I couldn't do it. I got upset and told her she didn't know what I was capable of."

"That's what Marsha overheard you say," I added, "But we thought it was a threat."

"I would never threaten her." He looked at Russell.

"Why didn't you tell the police when you heard she was dead?" I asked.

"I should have contacted the police. I feared that our recent argument and phone call would make me a suspect if foul play was involved…and then when I got here and saw Steve with a gun, I panicked. I fell down the stairs. Hoping to find some help, I hid here, in the casket room. When I saw Steve stagger into the room and Melody push him into a coffin, I must have fainted."

"That was the thud I heard. I've never been glad someone was late for an appointment with me before," I walked over and gently grabbed his hand.

"Now that we are okay, me too. I'm going to put off my estate planning for now. I'm not ready to leave this world anytime soon." His hands tightly gripped the sides of the stretcher.

"Me neither. Neither of us are going anywhere, anytime soon."

I looked down at his pant leg. A paramedic had cut the material away, exposing a swollen and cut right leg. "It appears I've broken my leg," he said.

Arthur Snugg stood behind several officers. He pushed his way forward.

"Mr. Snugg, I'm really, really sorry about your clock."

"What happened to my beloved clock?" Snugg raced out of the casket room toward the stairs.

"You might want to send a medic up after him," I told Russell.

"My clock, my clock!" Screams could be heard from the upper level of the funeral home.

Russell reached over and pulled me toward him.

"I was trying to do my civic duty," I said, collapsing into him.

"Only you, Melody Shore." Russell looked around the room. "I vote we get out of here."

Once we were outside, Russell walked over to his police cruiser. He returned with his hands behind his back, a big smile on his face.

"I got you a surprise." From behind his back, he pulled a small black and white kitten. "I want you to meet your new roommate."

"Oh Russell, he's adorable, but I can't have a kitten in my apartment." I scratched under the kitten's chin.

"Yes, you can. I went to the shelter earlier today with a lost dog and your landlord, John, was dropping off this new kitten."

"He was?"

"He said he found the little guy under his big maple out back."

"What about his dog, Duke?" The kitten purred and rubbed his head on my hand.

"Yeah, Duke was barking like crazy, and the kitty lay there, unafraid."

"Doesn't John want to keep him?"

"We got to talking, and I told him what an animal lover you are. We both agreed everyone should have a pet—even tough girls." Russell handed him to me.

"I can keep him? In my apartment?" I hugged the kitten to my chest.

"Yeah, John can visit him—with your permission, of course."

"Of course!"

The kitten buried his head into the crevice of my arm.

"I think you have a friend there, Clutch. What are you naming him?"

"I think Shady sounds perfect."

Arthur Snugg stepped over to us accompanied by Alex and J.J.

"Melody, I've talked to the police. I'm so grateful you are okay."

"Even though...your clock?" I handed Shady to Russell.

"The clock I can replace." Snugg smiled. "You, I can't."

"I feel the same way about you, Mr. Snugg." I gently touched his arm.

"Here, we ate your half, but we felt bad." Alex produced a white bakery box from behind his back.

"You wanted more," J.J. interjected.

"Yeah, but anyway, we bought a whole cake, so we're giving the rest to you, Melody," Alex handed me the mangled pastry box.

"Thanks, guys. I could use cake right now."

The next day, as I sat talking to Mr. Snugg about making cold calls to sell funeral plots, my mother called.

"Hi, Honey. Did you get to help Marsha?"

"Yes, Mom, I made the calls for Marsha."

"Did you get anyone to come out?" my mother asked.

"Well...two of the candidates showed up and one tried to kill me."

"Oh, Melody, don't be so dramatic."

"Don't worry, I locked myself in a casket and caught the bad guy. So, I don't have to worry about having claustrophobia."

"Oh, that's wonderful, dear. I have another book that's perfect for you. It's called, *Digging Through the Dirt to Find Your True Love.*"

"Huh? Why would I want that?"

"It's a real page turner. I've already picked up the sequel, *The Bare Bones Approach to Spotting a Shady Relationship.*"

"I think I'm good, Mom. There will be no shady relationship in my life...well, except my new cat, Shady!" ❦

Down the mahogany staircase walked Arthur Snugg dressed in black pants and a red jacket with large, intricately stitched cuffs and lapels....He wore a blood-red ascot and carried a devil's pitchfork.

Things Can't Get Any Hearse

*In the Garden of Peace, which was the closest garden to the funeral home, her body
lay face down, her head several inches from a tombstone.*

"Is she?" I stopped. I couldn't say another word.

*"Yes, Melody, she's dead," Kenneth said, pulling out the caution tape from a bag
he carried.*

An ambulance pulled into the lot as Kenneth, and I stood there in silence.

The EMTs exited their vehicle and turned the body over.

They cut her costume and began CPR.

*There she lay, dressed in her last costume, her ash-blond hair softly framing her
face. The Peaceful Rest umbrella lay open on the ground, partially sheltering her. Her
black corset still wrapped around her slender waist. Her heels glistening in the grass.
She would never dance in those heels again.*

Russell sped into the lot in his police cruiser.

"Oh, Russell, who could have done this?" I cried.

Russell and I stood at the window of my apartment looking out at the
fall leaves that covered my driveway and stuck to the wet windshield
and hood of my jeep, "Blue Betty." Last evening, a southerly weather
pattern had blown in, causing an unseasonably warm late-October morning
in our small town of Pleasantview, Pennsylvania. I really didn't need to warm
up my jeep, but I was like a kid with a new toy. I had to play with it immediately.

"I can't believe the deal I got on this remote start." I hit the button and
watched as Blue Betty came to life.

Russell wrapped his flannel shirt covered arms around me. The warmth of the flannel, the strength in his muscular arms, and his cologne were intoxicating.

"After Snugg's costume party Friday night, don't make any other plans for the weekend," he whispered in my ear before turning me around and laying a series of hot and heavy kisses on me.

"You seem a lot happier about going now than when I asked you last week." I gazed up into his tantalizing brown eyes. "You never come to any of my work things. I mean, I wouldn't expect you at the viewings or funerals, but you're so agreeable to going to tomorrow night's party."

"Oh, really," he said, breaking into a devilish grin. "Who is Sandy Fisher, again?" he asked, changing the subject.

"She's Snugg's new love interest." I sighed. "And the queen of strange parties," I added.

"That man changes women more than you change outfits," Russell said as I unwove my fingers from his and twirled in my burnt-orange polka-dot retro dress.

"She owns a costume shop out on Rt. 50. She dresses sultry in a lot of red and black." I fluttered my eyes at Russell.

"Oh, the gorgeous but dangerous type." Russell smiled.

"Yeah, and get this, you know how Snugg loves grandfather clocks? She collects pendulums. Everything from necklaces to gigantic clock ones."

"A common interest," Russell said.

"She gave him a desktop pendulum. It swings back and forth all day in his office. And there are pendulums tattooed all over her body...at least the parts I can see." I ran my finger across Russell's rock-solid chest. "The party is her idea," I added.

"Snugg think this is the one?" Russell asked.

"He's been dating her for three weeks now, and she decided that a costume party at the funeral home is the thing to do. Can you believe it?"

"Actually, no."

"There's something about a party at a funeral home that brings people out, even if it is simply because they are curious."

"I know I'm dying to go," Russell replied and then winked.

"Speaking of dying, it's almost eight-thirty. I have to get to work." I opened the refrigerator to see what I could take for lunch.

"I put the last of your homemade wedding soup in a bowl for you.

Why don't you take that?" Russell said, reaching into the refrigerator and proudly handing the container to me.

"It's going to be so romantic," I said as I gazed at the setting sun tinting the skyline a beautiful orange, blue, and yellow. It was in colorful competition with the trees lining Fifth Street dressed in a kaleidoscope of reds.

"This door never seems to shut tight anymore." My best friend, Claire, tugged hard as she locked the door to Claire's Cottage, her vintage clothing shop. "I love our Thursday night E&R's. Sorry I missed last week," Claire said, turning to me.

"Eat and Recap. Claire, you've picked up my abbreviation lingo."

"I have, haven't I?" Claire laughed.

"I can't wait for Russell to see me in this flapper costume you loaned me for the party." I peeked into the bag I was carrying containing the costume.

"You'll look super in it and Russell is going to make a great mobster with the fedora hat I gave you," Claire said.

"Isn't it terrific that Russell schedules himself on Thursday evenings now? You and I get our girl time and his weekends are mostly free for me."

"What did you say a minute ago when I was trying to lock the door, Melody?" she asked as we walked down Fifth Street toward the Corner Cupboard. The Corner Cupboard is a real-deal diner, and their food is really delicious.

"Russell has been acting mysterious this whole week. This could be it! I would definitely want a fall wedding." I scooped up a pile of fallen leaves, threw them up in the air, and began to twirl underneath them as they floated toward the ground.

"You think he's going to propose?" Claire stopped me mid-twirl and spun me around to face her.

"I don't know, maybe. Just last week, he said he hates costume parties. But this morning, he seemed excited to go to the one Snugg is throwing tomorrow night at The Peaceful Rest." I held out my left hand with its empty ring finger.

"When it happens, are you going to ask Snugg to walk you down the aisle?" Claire asked.

"I know it's strange, but probably. He is my boss, and he was my dad's best friend. He would probably say yes…and it's just like I always pictured when I was a young girl."

"Marrying a police officer?" Claire stopped to look into the window of Skip's Hardware. "You're lucky to have Russell. I really need to get a new set of locks for the store."

"I really am lucky! What I meant, though, was getting engaged at a costume party like my parents."

"I remember you telling me your parents got engaged at a costume party, but I didn't know it was a costume party at the funeral home. I'm sorry–I have to say it, Melody—that's weird and creepy."

"No. It wasn't at the funeral home, Claire! My parents got engaged outside a masquerade ball party in the courtyard of a fancy hotel in Pittsburgh."

"Does Russell know how your parents got engaged?" Claire asked as she held open the door to the Corner Cupboard allowing another young, in-love couple to exit.

"I told him once when we were watching this romantic comedy. The guy dropped to one knee and proposed to a girl wearing a masquerade mask. Russell was half-asleep though. Romantic movies aren't really his thing."

Claire and I found an empty booth. An attentive waiter came right over and we ordered apple cider margaritas, loaded nachos, and an appetizer plate of cheese sticks and fried zucchini to share.

"I remember the movie you were talking about," Claire said, taking a drink of her margarita. "But didn't the girl switch her mask with her twin so she could do a little convo to confront the twin's cheating boyfriend? The poor guy proposed to the wrong twin."

"Oh…I didn't watch the end. Besides, we're not wearing masks. I don't know what will happen, but Russell sure has been acting mysterious. He said he planned something for after, but he won't say what."

"Oh, sure, I can see the similarities," Claire said. She reached across the table and lightly tapped my forehead. "Just checking to see if my long-time bestie is still in there."

Everything about Friday morning was drab, except my mood. The temperature had dropped twenty degrees, the wind was testing Mother Nature's lung capacity, and a cold, steady rain fell. I sat holed up in my small glass-walled office daydreaming of dresses as I stared out into the dull-colored, silent funeral home.

Arthur Snugg and Sandy Fisher burst through the door, shaking the rain from their matching black trench coats.

"Mr. Snugg," I called, jumping up from my chair. "It's Friday morning! Tonight is the party." I looked down at my white oversized cable-knit sweater and skirt. I hadn't realized I had dressed in all white.

"Speaking of which, Melody, we would like you to go to Sandy's store and pick up our costumes and decorations." Arthur Snugg took Sandy Fisher's hand and together they glided through the lobby past a large peace lily and into my office.

As they stood in the doorway of my office, Arthur Snugg looking expectantly at me, his statement sank in.

"You want me to go to Ms. Fisher's store and pick up your costumes and decorations? Me?" I repeated Snugg's words as I applied new color-code tabs to my "Buried in Details" agenda. "From her store?" I looked from Arthur Snugg to Sandy Fisher, my eyes questioning.

"Yes, and please order the alcohol," Sandy said as she laid an "An Evening to Die For" alcohol brochure on top of my catalog of prayer cards. "This is my chosen bartender service for this evening."

"You want me to order the alcohol too?" I began to leaf through the brochure, stopping at a page of celebratory sparkling wines that caught my eye. "Pick up decorations, order alcohol—is this my party or hers?" I whispered under my breath.

"And tell the bar service to bill me," Snugg said. "We make a great team, the three of us." Arthur Snugg smiled, his eyes expectantly wide. He pulled a $200 check written out to me, Melody Shore, from his suitcoat pocket and dangled it over my desk. "The check is for you. A little bonus for yourself. I think you deserve it." He placed the check in my hand. "You might have some expenses coming up. This will help, I'm sure," he added.

"I will! I mean, wow, thanks. I can pick up your costumes and decorations and order alcohol, if it helps you, Mr. Snugg." Then I turned to Sandy Fisher. "Russell isn't a champagne drinker, so a good sparkling wine will be great for toasting tonight."

"It's a triple play for the offense, my love," Snugg said, his eyes laser-focused on Sandy. He wrapped his arm around her slender waist as his eyes traveled down to her voluptuous pendulum-decorated chest. "Melody here is a big baseball fan."

"Oh, I would love to hear more about that." Sandy Fisher strutted into the funeral home lobby. She fluffed her perfectly styled hair, pulled out her pocket mirror, touched up her hot red lipstick, and reapplied her dark eyeliner. Her mirror must have caught the reflection of Walt Hart, the dead body laid out in the Rose Room waiting for his eleven o'clock eulogy service, because she abruptly turned and walked back to my office. Sandy Fisher snuggled up close to Arthur Snugg and fluttered her thick fake lashes at him.

"Actually, Mr. Snugg, a triple play benefits the defense, not the offense." I folded the check and placed it in my crocodile handbag.

The happy couple quickly headed up to Snugg's office to continue their love fest. I called *An Evening to Die For*, and ordered top shelf liquor, an assortment of beer, and five bottles of sparkling wine. Three bottles would probably be plenty, but I was sure Mr. Snugg wouldn't mind me taking any leftover unopened wine to my celebration afterward.

Walt Hart's service and burial kept my mind off the evening's party for the entire morning. His current wife, three ex-wives with their current husbands, and his eight children all tried to sit in the front row, which consisted of six chairs. They drew cards to see who would claim the front row and a fight broke out when wife number two accused wife number one of fixing the deck. Then, the man who was to sing hymns accompanied by the deceased's cousin on acoustic guitar came down with laryngitis, and the family insisted I sing instead. When I thought things couldn't get any worse, the lights in the Rose Room went out just as the minister was saying, "Into the darkness a righteous man will never go." I found several candles and the service continued until the power returned.

After that fiasco of a funeral, I went in search of Arthur Snugg's twin nephews, Alex and J.J., to enlist their help picking up Snugg and Sandy Fisher's costumes and decorations.

"Look at this, Mel, the relatives of the guy we just buried left us a cookie tray and this note," J.J. said when I entered the family room. The family room is reserved for families to gather between viewings and has a small kitchenette, a large round table and chairs, and two recliners. Alex and J.J. were both reclining.

J.J. jumped up and waved a thank-you note in front of my face. I grabbed it from his hand.

"The sweetness you have shown our family crumbled our hearts. The family of Walter Hart."

"We really need to keep a carton of milk on hand for times like these." J.J. opened the refrigerator and peered in. Alex looked up from his gaming magazine, grabbed a chocolate chip cookie, and shoved it in his mouth.

"We better get going," I said to Alex and J.J. "The party starts at seven tonight, and we have to be ready."

The rain had stopped. I put on my tortoiseshell sunglasses and pulled the visor down in Blue Betty to keep out the sun's glare. I drove Alex and J.J. out of Pleasantview, and down Route 50 towards Sandy Fisher's store, Costumes Galore.

"Do you see a costume shop?" I asked them as we approached the address. "Your uncle said her store was in a mall, but it isn't what I pictured." I pulled Blue Betty into the nearly empty strip mall parking lot.

"Looks like that is it, over there. *Costumes Galore*. See that big warehouse building right next to Pizza Palace?" J.J. rolled his window down pointing toward the most deserted area of the strip mall.

I drove closer and parked in front of the store. A neon sign that read "Costumes Galore–OPEN" hung above a single glass door. Next to the door sat two skeletons in lawn chairs. Each held a sign advertising that all décor was 50% off.

"We'll wait out here, Melody," Alex said.

"I'm thinking pizza," J.J. added.

"I didn't bring you two along to party in the parking lot." I got out and started to walk to the door. Neither twin moved. "If you are staying here until needed, stay by my jeep and don't run it or change my radio station," I said over my shoulder as I walked into the store alone.

Costumes, decorations, and accessories filled the walls and racks. Blue veiled lanterns on poles placed at the end of each aisle crackled with an eerie glow. Pop culture mannequins and creepy horror characters stood on guard throughout the store. Two machine-gun-strapped mannequins framed both sides of a door marked "Office," and two devil-dressed characters stood beside a door marked "Stairway to Hell." It looked like Halloween and the dark world had exploded inside the warehouse.

A witch's cackling and the sound of a bubbling pot played on repeat.

A 50-something-year-old woman with teased-toward-the-sky, flaming red hair, and fiery green eyes resembling Madame Medusa, sat behind a large counter with a glass display case jam-packed with accessories. She was on her cellphone.

"Sandy, you don't want to see me angry," Madame Medusa shouted. She quickly hung up, adjusted her large dangling blue earrings, and turned her eyes to me.

"I'm picking up costumes and decorations for the owner," I yelled over the witch's cackle.

"I'm the store owner, Linda Hines," she said, looking me up and down as if she were sizing me up to replace my white sweater outfit with something on display in the store. Please don't let her suggest the Bride of Frankenstein costume, I silently prayed.

"They send angels now to pick up the devil's décor. Or perhaps you're an angel who has lost her wings?" She grinned so wide that her thick bright red lipstick marked her front teeth. "We have some in aisle three."

"Do I have the wrong store? I was told Sandy Fisher owns this store." I looked around. The décor certainly matched Sandy.

"We're partners," she answered flatly. "You must mean for the party we're hosting tonight at a funeral home. Give me a few minutes." She disappeared behind a curtained wall without another word.

I stood still for several minutes, only turning my head when a cackle or scream burst from one of the displays. Then, curiosity took over. I walked up and down the aisles, admiring in an almost horrified way the assortment of decorations. There were dragons who billowed smoke with the touch of their tails, assorted stuffed black birds marked down to seventy-give percent off, and true to Sandy Fisher, an entire wall of swinging pendulums. I stopped at a display of glowing necklaces and tried several on.

I checked my watch. Fifteen minutes had gone by. Linda Hines had not returned.

"I will be right back," I hollered, my voice the cheeriest sound in the room.

Outside the store, Alex and J.J. leaned against Blue Betty. Two very attractive women had joined their stakeout and the four of them were eating from a box of pizza that sat atop Blue Betty's hood.

"Hey, Mel, we saved you a slice." J.J. held up the pizza box.

"I would like you to meet Kimberly, my date for tonight's party." Alex motioned toward the girl with light brown skin and pixie-cut black hair.

"And this is my date, Chelsea," J.J. said, taking a large sidestep and planting himself next to the girl with long blond hair, large blue eyes, and lips painted with pink pout lip liner.

Both women were dressed casually in sweaters, jeans, and boots.

"You're bringing dates? Tonight?" I looked from one twin to the other. "I need you to help with the party."

"This is Melody. The girl we've been telling you about," Alex said. "Uncle A is a mortician and owns the funeral home that is hosting tonight's party. Melody here, she keeps everything running smooth."

"That's hysterical," Kimberly said. "We work at the costume store and keep everything running." Kimberly motioned to Costumes Galore.

"Smooth," Chelsea added, smiling at J.J.

"Let's go inside and find us some costumes." Kimberly grabbed Alex by the hand and we all followed them into the costume store.

Alex stepped up to the counter to Linda Hines. She had finally come out from behind the curtain, but she was back on her phone. An assortment of decorations piled in boxes and a black costume bag lay across the accessory counter.

Alex pulled Snugg's business card out of his pocket. "Snugg's Peaceful Rest Funeral Home and Cemetery. People are dying to spend eternity with us," he said, reading the card. He and J.J. nodded in unison at the girls.

"Our Uncle A. His girlfriend is Sandy Fisher. We came to pick every-thing up for her party." Alex attempted to hand the card to Linda Hines.

"The only thing she ever does herself is solicit men to have parties," Linda Hines shrieked at Alex. Then she screamed into her cell phone. "That's right, you heard me, Sandy, I do all the real work. I started this business and brought you along, rent free." She stormed out the door, hollering back to Kimberly and Chelsea, "I need you two to work until six p.m."

"Of course, you do," Kimberly and Chelsea both answered.

J.J. pulled four ninja turtle costumes down from a rack and held them up. "How about these for the four of us, tonight?"

"Cowabunga!" Alex said, taking them from his hand.

"I think you two have found the perfect dates," I said, pressing a but-ton and activating the music on two banjo-playing skeleton decorations whose eyes glowed red and heads rotated in unison as they strummed their banjos.

Alex and J.J. opened Blue Betty's tailgate, put down part of the back seat, and loaded three large boxes in.

"Take these swords back inside," I said to Alex. "They extend the entire length of my jeep. We can't take them."

He gave me a dejected look and then he and J.J. went back into the store. Out they came carrying a three-foot coffin, which they attempted to hoist it onto Blue Betty's roof rack.

"Absolutely not! We have enough coffins at the funeral home," I said.

The boys returned the coffin to the store and came back this time only carrying one small box. J.J. draped Arthur Snugg and Sandy Fisher's cos-tumes over the larger boxes and he and Alex jumped in. Alex held the small box on his lap in the front seat.

I climbed in the driver's seat and turned the key. She made a single clicking noise.

"I think my battery is dead! This can't be happening! I have to call Jim's Jeeps." I checked my watch. "The party starts in three hours!"

I started to dial Jim's Jeeps when Arthur Snugg rumbled into the lot in his muffler-less hearse followed by Sandy Fisher in her red Mercedes.

I jumped out of Blue Betty.

"Mr. Snugg, Blue Betty is dead!"

"Where's her body? Is there a death certificate?" Arthur Snugg peered into Blue Betty's open window.

"Mr. Snugg, I need a vehicle to get back and ready for tonight's party!"

"Here's the key to the hearse. You can use that." He removed a single silver key from his key ring. "I'll take it for repairs another day. We will drive the boys back."

Alex and J.J. climbed out of my jeep and stood admiring Sandy Fisher's car.

I quickly dialed Jim's Jeeps. "Sorry, we're closed. It's a family wedding," the recording played on repeat.

"The hearse? You want me to drive the hearse back?"

"Maybe gas." Arthur Snugg said.

"You think it's empty?" I asked.

"Not the hearse."

"No! Who's in it?" I gasped.

"No one is in it. I thought you were referring to the full gas tank." Arthur Snugg patted my shoulder. "Take the hearse, it will be fine." Alex, J.J., and Arthur Snugg quickly removed the boxes and the costume bag from Blue Betty and piled them in the front of the hearse.

"Put up the decorations, I'm short on time," Sandy Fisher hollered over her shoulder as she, Arthur Snugg, Alex and J.J. walked toward Costume Galore.

"Okay, 'Creeper Keeper,' you're all I got. No stiff competition." I lightly touched the hearse's black hood. I just need you to take me back.

I climbed into the box-filled front of the hearse and for lack of room, I held the smallest box in my lap. "The curtains can't close on me now. Tonight has to be perfect," I said as I pulled open the drape that separated the driver seat and the rear of the hearse. A coffin lay in the back.

"What the hell! Snugg said it was empty!" I drove out of the parking lot like an ambulance driver.

When I arrived back at the funeral home, the catering company was busy bringing in cheese and olive platters, sugar-glazed ham, chicken on skewers, deviled eggs, and oysters Rockefeller. Vinaigrette and Caesar dips sat next to the artfully displayed crudité cups.

In the first box from Costumes Galore were caldrons and two mini pendulum card holders filled with 10% off coupons for Sandy Fisher's store. I carefully filled the cauldrons with dry ice the caterer had brought. Once I activated them with hot water, they gave off a mood-setting effect. I set one of the pendulum card holders on a table in the foyer and another in the family room in between the microwave and the wall.

The second box contained several masked head forms. I tried my best to hide the heads behind flowers, but it made the heads appear even spookier. What is she thinking, sending fake body parts to a funeral home? Where are the glittery pumpkins, gourds, and cornstalk displays?

I went to the hearse and carried in the last two boxes. The large one contained black and purple lights and a fog machine. I set up the fog machine and draped the lights throughout the funeral home, plugging them in as I went.

I was holding the contents of the small box when Arthur Snugg, Sandy Fisher, and the twins arrived.

"It's a Bluetooth speaker," Sandy Fisher said, taking the black skull adorned with pink sunglasses from my hand. She pressed a few buttons and dance party songs filled the air.

"Everything looks wonderful, Melody. Sandy, you have created a real party atmosphere," Arthur Snugg said.

"Can you guys quit dancing and place these cocktail tables strategically around the funeral home?" I asked Alex and J.J., who were breakdancing in and out of the mist created by the fog machine.

Satisfied everything looked good, or as good as it could with Sandy's decorating taste, I went into the bathroom and changed into my silver flapper costume complete with choker, matching feather headband, a boa, and cigarette holder.

At seven p.m., the front doors of the funeral home opened, and the guests arrived.

An Elvis impersonator took off his bird-winged cape and handed it to me. "Thank you, thank you very much," he said. He wore a white jumpsuit and large sequined belt.

Two guests dressed as tourists in matching striped shirts, khaki pants, and floppy hats walked in with cameras around their necks and carrying luggage. They set their luggage down directly in front of the food tables and began to take photos of each other and the funeral home.

"The vacation of a lifetime," the tourist woman gushed to her counterpart. "I could stay here with you forever."

I quickly pushed their luggage to a corner.

George Bush and Kiss mingled with vampires, warlocks, and Batman.

Down the mahogany staircase walked Arthur Snugg and Sandy Fisher both dressed in black and red. The prince and princess of darkness. Arthur Snugg had on black pants and a red jacket with large, intricately stitched cuffs and lapels, all in black. He wore a blood-red ascot and carried a devil's pitchfork. Sandy Fisher wore a red miniskirt dress, a red and black fitted cape, and black suede boots that extended over her knee to her thigh. A laced up black corset wrapped around her slender body. She strutted with a skull walking-stick.

"Her boots are killer," I said to Russell, who stood beside me in his fedora hat and pinstriped suit, looking like the handsomest mob man I had ever seen.

"Those four-inch heels could be weapons," Russell said, nuzzling my neck with kisses.

The party was going strong, and Russell and I were dancing to "Just the Way You Are" and making memories, when his phone rang.

"Mel, I'm really sorry. I have to go into the station. You got everything under control here." He glanced around the guest-filled lobby. "An hour at the most until I return."

"Russell, you're leaving now?" I looked at my watch. It was eight twenty-five. "The life of a police officer's w...I mean, while you're gone, I'll make sure there is an extra wine opener we can borrow for later."

"No need. I can twist the cap off our beer."

"But I thought..."

He gave me a passionate kiss and hurried out into the rainy night.

The bartender motioned me over.

"The guy in the Dracula costume is really intoxicated. Do you know him?"

"Which one? There are four of them," I counted them out in the crowd with my long cigarette holder.

"Yeah, there must have been a sale on Dracula this year," the bartender replied.

"You mean the one attempting the cha-cha slide even though there is no music on right now?" I clapped my hands and stomped my feet on the floor in imitation.

"That would be the one," he said.

"A local politician, maybe? Our 'under the influence Dracula,' has to be someone of influence," I said, taking a sip of sparkling wine.

Approximately twenty guests mingled at the bar and danced in the fog-filled, light-strung lobby. In the Rose Room I could see the two tourists snapping photos of excited guests in front of a closed coffin. Every seat was occupied in the Lilac Room which had been turned into a chapel with Elvis strutting and gyrating in front of the pulpit. There were loud conversations and laughing.

Until the screaming started.

In the middle of the makeshift lobby dance floor, Sandy Fisher had pulled the crown and black wig off a regal skeleton queen, revealing the flaming red hair of her partner, Linda Hines.

"Money!" Sandy Fisher shouted. She guzzled her martini in one large gulp and sucked the olive down with a slurp. "You'll get your money over my dead body, Linda!"

"The warehouse isn't free rent!" Linda Hines screamed at Sandy. She picked up her black wig, threw it over one of the head forms that decorated a nearby table, put her crown back on her head, and paraded out the door.

Sandy Fisher turned to Kimberly who was dancing, beer in hand, across the dance floor. Her turtle shell shook perfectly in time to the beat of the music.

"And you...you and your cousin, you work for me. You don't attend my events," Sandy Fisher said.

"Fine, I quit. Drop dead," Kimberly said. She plunged her ninja sword into the sugar-glazed ham, burst into laughter, and walked down the stairs to the basement of the funeral home.

"You think we don't know what your game is," Chelsea said to Sandy.

"Someone needs to put a stop to you!" Chelsea followed Kimberly.

The funeral home was silent for a moment, and then the music started loudly again. The Queen of Darkness glided back onto the dance floor, motioning for Snugg to join her in a fast song.

Arthur Snugg swayed back and forth and slowly shook his head side to side. He turned and made his way over to me, holding onto the wall for support.

"Mel...Melody, let's hire Elvis! What do you think?" His glossy eyes drifted around the room.

"Mr. Snugg, how much have you had to drink?"

He held five fingers up and counted them before speaking again. "I haven't had fun since your dad asked me to be his best man. Snuggy...I mean Snuggs...that's what your dad called me." He put his hand on my shoulder for support. "I stand by you when you and bury, stand by me when I marry. Or something like that. Your dad was funny." We both laughed.

Several fast dance songs later, Sandy Fisher quit dancing alone and marched over to us.

"This is my party and you ruined it," Sandy Fisher said, circling and jabbing the skull head of her walking stick in my face.

"Me?" I asked.

"Yes, you! Stealing the show in your fancy flapper costume. You might work for Arthur, but I am who is important to him."

"Sandy, Melody is very important to me," Arthur Snugg said, his voice rising.

"Arthur, you're spineless and boring!" Sandy Fisher pushed Arthur Snugg. He stumbled backwards, lost his footing, and tripped on one of the dangling light strings, plunging the lobby into darkness. I raced over and fumbled around until I found the plug and turned the lights back on. Sandy Fisher threw her skull-topped walking stick down, grabbed a Peaceful Rest complimentary umbrella, and stormed toward the door.

"Sandy, come back!" Arthur Snugg said.

The funeral home door banged closed.

"I'm going to lay down," Snugg said to me. He picked up Sandy's walking stick, placed it in the corner of the lobby, and slowly walked back up his mahogany staircase into his office.

"The hosts of the party," I said to the bartender. "This kind of stuff happens all the time at The Peaceful Rest...Can I get a beer?"

"The craft beer is a popular item," he said, popping off the crown cap. "Do you want to be bartender? I can go to Beer Warehouse and pick up some more."

I looked behind the makeshift bar at the cooler of beer. There were only four left.

"I will get Mr. Snugg's nephews to go," I said, scanning the crowd for the Ninja Turtles. They were nowhere in sight. "I guess I will go get more beer," I said to no one, as the bartender was now busy with the group of Draculas who were downing shots and ordering more.

When I returned twenty minutes later from Beer Warehouse, drenched and lugging a case of beer, no one seemed to care that the guests of honor were MIA. The party was in full swing with Kiss leading the party train. The train weaved through the Rose Room and headed toward the Lilac Room where the dancers stopped and all chugged a cup of my sparkling wine.

Russell, Mr. Snugg, and the twins were nowhere in sight. I checked my phone. No messages from Russell. I fluffed up my rain-wet hair and climbed the stairs to Snugg's office.

"Mr. Snugg, why don't you come back down and enjoy the party?"

"I think I will have to break it off with Sandy," Arthur Snugg said as he pushed the pendulum back and forth on his desk.

"She certainly is making it easy," I said, giving him a hopeful smile.

My phone buzzed a message. It was Russell.

I should be there in about 10 minutes. Double red heart emoji.

"Mr. Snugg, come on, let's go back and enjoy our party."

As I hurried out of his office, Arthur Snugg picked the pendulum decoration up and put it in his desk drawer.

Back downstairs, drunken Dracula sat with George Bush and the latest rookie on Russell's force, Kenneth, in a row of our wingback chairs. Kenneth gestured for me to come over.

"Melody, I was down the street when the call came in, so I came right away," Kenneth said.

"Dwayne Levick, township mayor." George Bush took off his mask, revealing a middle-aged, bald-headed man. "I called the authorities, Ms. Shore, when my son, David here, came back telling me what he saw outside." He patted Drunk Dracula's leg. "Tell us what you saw, son."

"This party really bites," Drunk Dracula slurred. "I went outside to smoke in the bushes, and I saw a woman in a Garden of Pizza."

"The Garden of Peace? Is that what you mean?" I asked. "That's one of our sections in the cemetery," I said to Kenneth.

"Melody, can you come outside with me?" Kenneth asked. "We need someone to identify a body."

In the Garden of Peace, which is the closest garden to the funeral home, her body lay face down, her head several inches from a tombstone.

"Is she?" I stopped. I couldn't say another word.

"Yes, Melody, she's dead," Kenneth said, pulling out caution tape from a bag he carried.

An ambulance pulled into the lot as Kenneth, and I stood there in silence.

The EMTs exited their vehicle and turned the body over. They cut her costume and began CPR.

There she lay, dressed in her last costume, her ash-blond hair softly framing her face. The Peaceful Rest umbrella lay open, partially sheltering her. Her black corset still wrapped around her slender waist. Her four-inch heels glistening in the grass. She would never dance in those heels again.

Russell sped into the lot in his police cruiser.

"Oh, Russell, who could have done this?" I cried out as they placed a sheet over Sandy Fisher.

"Keep everyone back, Mel, please." Russell gestured to the crowd that was now standing around us.

"Russell, this wet grass is all plowed down," I pointed to the grass slightly beyond Sandy Fisher.

"It looks like someone hit her with a car and she flew into this tombstone," the mayor said.

"Oh, how awful!" I looked at the shocked faces of the crowd of guests. "Where did the person go?"

"Didn't you just return with beer?" the questioning bartender asked. "You had to have seen something."

Kenneth roped off the scene and he and Russell started their work gathering evidence.

"Sandy, oh, Sandy." Arthur Snugg's usual authoritative tone had turned into a mere whisper.

The mayor put his arm around Snugg and guided him back into the funeral home.

Back inside the funeral home, Russell and Kenneth separated and questioned us.

"What is your relationship with Sandy Fisher, and did you leave the funeral home for any reason tonight?" they asked each of us.

"Kimberly and I were downstairs in my office. The craft beer was low. I keep a six-pack chilled for times like tonight." I heard Alex plead his case to Kenneth. The two of them sat across from one another in the Lilac Room, now turned Interrogation Room.

"J.J. and I did go out in his truck to be alone. The funeral home was freaking me out," Chelsea said to Russell.

"I don't look good in stripes. I'm a plaid kind of guy," J.J. whined. He ran his hands over his buzz-cut blondish hair and then tightly gripped the buttons on his green Henley shirt as he paced back and forth in front of the Rose Room.

"My license is suspended," Kimberly said.

"I don't drive," Chelsea said to Kenneth. "We took a bus here."

"Yes, I took her photo, but we don't hardly even know her," the tourist dressed woman answered.

"Keep the photos, we don't want them now," her husband said, handing his and his wife's camera over to Kenneth.

"I won't speak without my attorney present," Elvis said, his hands tightly gripping his large belt buckle.

"Yes, Sandy and I had a fight," Arthur Snugg said through gritted teeth. He took off his red jacket and sat down on the mahogany staircase.

"Did you chase after her?" Kenneth asked, taking notes.

"No, I went up to my office to lie down after she left." He pointed up the staircase with his pitchfork. "Melody can verify that. She came up to talk to me. What kind of man do you think I am? Sandy was my girlfriend." Arthur Snugg stood up and then sat back down. "Can I have some ibuprofen and water?"

"The people I saw leave were the deceased, the redhead, two turtles and Ms. Shore," the bartender said. "I'm off duty, Snugg. Get your own water. This is the first and last funeral party I will tend."

"Yes, I did leave ten minutes after Sandy did. I went to get beer," I said to Russell who was interrogating me alone in my office. "I remember checking my watch when I returned. You weren't back and it was twenty-five after nine," I added sourly.

"Did you see anything or anyone else in the parking lot?" Russell asked, reaching for my hand.

"It was raining so hard. I could barely see to drive," I said, pulling away and hugging myself.

Kenneth interrupted Russell's interrogation of me to inform him that the rain had dampened the efforts to retrieve any evidence of tire type from the soaked grass.

"Mel, why did you even go out in such weather?" Russell then asked.

"I thought these people would drink the hard liquor. And the sparkling wine is for our toast. Was for our toast..." I burst into tears.

"Our toast?" Russell looked at me with questioning eyes.

"This was to be our perfect night!" I cried out.

"Kenneth, please go check the hearse for any damage." Russell closed his notebook and said, "Mel, I know this evening is ruined, but I'll make it up to you. The weekend isn't over."

He walked out into the lobby. "Where is Linda Hines?"

"I told you, she left earlier," the bartender said.

"I'm aware of that, sir. Now please sit back down. We will send an officer to question her in the morning." Russell paced back and forth as he talked on the phone to his commanding officer.

Kenneth appeared five lonely minutes later.

"There is no damage, Sarge, to the hearse, not even a ding."

"Melody couldn't have hit her, then." Arthur Snugg pounded his pitchfork down on the floor in approval and then quickly dropped it. He covered his eyes with his hands and sighed.

"What about J.J.'s truck?" Russell asked.

"No damage to J.J.'s truck, either." Kenneth said to Russell. "It couldn't have been Melody or J.J."

"You are all free to leave, but don't plan on taking any trips anytime soon," Russell said. He started to walk toward me, but I was too upset to talk to him. I grabbed my coat and hurried out the door to the hearse.

Russell called my phone as soon as I pulled out of the funeral home lot. I let it go to voicemail:

Mel, I am so sorry I had to question you. I had big plans for this weekend. I know how excited you have been about accessorizing Blue Betty. There is a car show over in Foxmoor this weekend. I got us a bed and breakfast and until tonight, I had plans to take you there. Please call me back.

"I thought he was going to propose!" I slowly drove home, my sobs the only sound in the silent hearse.

I tossed and turned all night, my dreams filled with Russell arresting me, and the draculas from the party acting as my judge and jurors. Unable to sleep, I got out of bed. Darkness blanketed the early morning sky and filled my heart. I knew I had to clear my name and my co workers' names. Worst of all, I went from thinking I was getting engaged to being a suspect in a murder. At least the hearse was off the suspect list. I got in and drove to the costume store in search of clues.

When I arrived at Costumes Galore, the parking lot was empty and dimly lit, but lights shone brightly inside the store. I pulled on the door and hurried inside. The store was in shambles. The accessory counter was ripped apart. The counter drawer contents were strewn about on the floor. Linda Hines sat on the floor with a large stack of papers surrounding her.

"What are you doing here?" Linda Hines asked as she pushed a piece of paper through a large shredder next to her.

"That's a strange thing to be doing after your business partner just died," I blurted out.

Linda stood up, fire in her eyes.

She picked an accessory sword off the ground and ran at me with it. I dodged out of her path, and she smashed headfirst into a wall of costumes. I scrambled to find something to defend myself. In the process, I pulled the head off a display dummy and when I threw it at her, it missed and activated the store's light display and audio system. "I'm an empty soul," repeated over and over as strobe orange and purple lights lit up the store's walls.

Linda Hines untangled herself, ripped a Wonder Woman cape off her head, and lunged at me again.

"She left me no choice! She was spending all our profits on herself," Linda Hines screamed. "This store is mine now!" She dove forward at me.

On the third lunge, I caught her arm and knocked her to the ground. The sword fell from her hand and hit the ground with a thud.

Linda Hines ran toward the doorway marked "Stairway to Hell." She flung open the door and raced down the steps.

I ran after her down the wooden stairs. The basement of Costumes Galore was a maze of boxes. Linda Hines ran through them, knocking them in my way as she ran. Boxes hit the ground and burst open, revealing mannequin parts, stuffed crows with glassy eyes, and hangers. Visions of fighting her with mannequin arm parts or hurling a crow at her flashed in my mind. I picked up a mess of tangled hangers as I ran after her. Any weapon is better than no weapon.

Then I saw it: An old gray Chevy Blazer with the cracked front bumper. "Whose car is that?" I shouted.

As I ran toward Linda's mid-size SUV, she rolled up the downed window. I swung the hangers, catching her mid-roll, but she threw the car into reverse, and I had to jump back to keep from getting run over. She backed right through the closed garage door–the trailing jumble of hangers flew from the Blazer like bullets.

Linda drove erratically through the parking lot, laying tire and spinning around. I carefully brushed myself off and stood up, avoiding the splintered wood, glass glittering in the morning light. When I heard Linda gun the engine in the distance, I knew she was headed back in my direction. Spotting concrete steps to the upper parking lot, I raced toward them.

I barely jumped into the driver's side of the hearse as Linda fled the scene. Suddenly, Arthur Snugg's brown PT Cruiser pulled into the lot.

"Sandy stole from me, Melody!" Snugg leaned in through my window slightly out of breath. "When Russell searched her bag, he found my money clip...the one...when you and I went to a baseball game together."

"Get in, Mr. Snugg, and hold on." Snugg pocketed the money clip as he slid in and buckled his seat belt.

Linda Hines' Blazer was disappearing down Route 50, so I stomped my foot down as hard as I could on the pedal. The hearse's speedometer reached seventy miles per hour.

"Get her, Melody," Arthur Snugg said, his hands on the dashboard, jaw set in determination.

We started down a hill and a sharp bend appeared. Linda Hines slowed down and the hearse careened past her. I jammed down hard on the brake, but the hearse went into a slide. I turned a hard left and steered out of it.

That's when the back door flew open. A wooden casket–complete with a skeleton that had been put in the hearse for the party as a joke–ejected out of the back and slid out like a cannon. It hit the ground. In the review mirror, we saw it splinter apart. The skeleton broke into pieces and landed at the foot of a nearby tree.

The hearse and debris completely blocked the road.

Linda's Blazer skidded to a stop. She jumped from her SUV and began to run. Snugg ran after her and tackled her. The two of them landed on the skeleton and were in a one-skeleton, two-person wrestling match, until I joined in. Together, we got her hands behind her back and I cuffed her.

"Why do you have handcuffs?" she snarled.

"A gift from Russell. He said a girl like me should always be prepared," I said as I snapped the cuffs around Linda Hines' wrists. Arthur Snugg looked at me with appreciation.

"I should have never gone into business with her," Linda Hines confessed as I pulled her to her feet. "I came back to the party to try and make her see things my way. She was standing there glaring at me when I pulled into the lot, and I swerved and hit her."

"You have more than skeletons in your closet," I said, pulling on a bone that had attached itself to her flaming red hair, making her look like a disheveled Pebbles Flintstone.

I was walking her toward the hearse when Russell and Kenneth pulled up in a cruiser. Kenneth took Linda Hines' arm and guided her toward the back seat. They drove off to the station.

"Mel, are you okay?" Russell asked and gently kissed me.

"How did you know where to find me?" I asked, wrapping my arms around him and hugging him back.

"We came as fast as we could when a call came through dispatch that a hearse was speeding down Route fifty in pursuit of a gray Blazer."

"We need to talk," Russell whispered in my ear.

My eyebrows raised.

"For right now, all I am going to say is you deserve something better to toast about than a car show."

Russell turned and shook Snugg's hand.

"Melody here is the hero," Arthur Snugg said.

"Thank you, Mr. Snugg. We are a good team," I answered and then turned to Russell. "Russell, Linda Hines just admitted she hit Sandy Fisher. We think Sandy Fisher stole from Mr. Snugg and possibly Linda's store, too." I motioned for Snugg to get back into the passenger side. "I can drive Mr. Snugg back and then tell you everything over breakfast, if you want."

"There isn't anything I want more," Russell said with a grin.

Monday morning at The Peaceful Rest, Arthur Snugg, Alex, J.J., and I gathered in my office.

"This whole thing is so upsetting, but I'm glad to know the truth, Melody." Arthur Snugg gave me a fatherly hug and continued. "And I am so glad I have you to rely on. I know The Peaceful Rest is in good hands with you next to me in the driver's seat."

Snugg then turned to the twins. "What about you two? Have you spoken to your dates?"

"Dinner Friday, Pizza Palace," J.J. answered. He and Alex high-fived.

"Oh, that reminds me," Arthur Snugg said. "Melody, this afternoon, please hold my calls. I have a consultation with a female guest from the party. If all goes well, I might invite her to dinner afterward." Snugg gave me a hopeful smile.

"Sure thing, Mr. Snugg. Oh, and Jim's Jeeps called. Blue Betty is fixed. I'm back where I belong, in her driver's seat." ♡

Next to the bar cart was my baking cupboard. I opened it and found an unopened bag of chocolate baking chips. If I hurried, I could whip up a batch of my Almost-Famous To-Die-For Chocolate Chip Bars for the party and be back to work in an hour.

Recipe for Murder

I wrapped a strand of silvery-white lights around a bare lamp-post that lined Main Street. "I love the holidays!" I said, brushing a gathering of snowflakes off my new leopard camo flats.

"Yeah, can you believe it's eight a.m. on a Friday and there must be over fifty townspeople out helping?" said my movie star-handsome boyfriend, Russell.

"When my mother called and tried to rope me into helping with the cleanup, I figured she wanted the pumpkins for free compost in her garden," I said.

"Well, she probably does, but your idea to recycle the pumpkins and cornstalks for Pleasantview's wildlife is a hit." Russell pointed down the street.

All along Main Street, merchant doors dripped with evergreen wreaths, the pungent scent curling up the sidewalks, and last but not least, hundreds of red bows.

Pleasantview, my hometown, is an interesting place. I realize that more and more, ever since I moved home eight months ago after a nasty break-up with a less than jolly soul. Who would have thought when I returned home, jobless and heartbroken, that I would enjoy arranging the ever-after, or that I would find love again?

Russell loaded two more small pumpkins onto the tailgate of an almost full township truck parked on Main Street. I picked up a cornstock tassel that the wind deposited at my feet and tickled the back of his neck.

"Keep your hands where I can see them," Russell joked as he reached for his handcuffs that hung from his police blues.

"Here, I got that, Mel." Russell plugged in a lighted snowflake with an extension cord and tucked the cord into the greenery around a light pole. "We're out of decorations. Let's go to breakfast."

"Only twenty-five more days!" I said, tying one of the last bows around my knit hat and putting my arm in his.

"Yep, I know. December first is finally here! You've had that holiday countdown calendar hanging up since before Thanksgiving," Russell said, putting his hands on my waist. We wove through the maze of crepe-filled decorations and wrap-happy pedestrians like a two-person train until we got to the corner of Eighth Street.

I turned around and looked back up the street while Russell held the door open to Marsha's Cafe. Through the glass door, Pleasantview looked like a picturesque holiday painting.

The restaurant was warm, the booth cozy, and Marsha had put springs of holly in the centerpiece of each table. Soon, we were settled with drinks. Steam escaped from my oversized mug. Thankfully, I was wearing my favorite vintage fall outfit, a cream blouse and burgundy skirt with retro-style pockets. Pockets come in handy for carrying that little bit of extra tape and wire on decorating day.

"The French toast looks good today, Deena," Russell said. Deena is Marsha's regular morning shift server.

"You're going to get the bear claw anyway, aren't you?" She deftly picked up Russell's menu and turned to me.

"This coffee is perfect," I said, handing my menu back.

"You didn't want your go-to breakfast?" Russell asked as his bear claw arrived. He pointed to my side of the table, empty of food. "What will Marsha say? She might tell your mother."

"I don't have time. I need to be early for work. Snugg ordered Christmas decorations for the funeral home, and guess who's putting them up?" I stole a bite of his bear claw.

Russell just smiled.

"Since we are talking about work," I continued, forcing a smile, "I feel bad that I can't make your department holiday party."

"I know, my diligent girlfriend can't let down her mortician boss. He needs to bury another body," Russell said.

"Wait a minute. You told me to stop in after the viewing because it wasn't going to be a big deal!"

"Fair enough. I thought it was going to be the same as last year..." Russell sighed.

"Pretzels, beer, and a double-elimination air hockey tournament in the no-window brick basement of the police station?" I asked.

"Air hockey is my game." Russell took another bite of his bear claw, and continued, "Yesterday Joan from dispatch said we should all dress up. Something about photos for a holiday card." Russell frowned. "I can't take myself seriously in a suit. I don't know how Snugg does it every day. He not only has to wear a suit, but he makes dead guys wear one too."

"Yeah, he's great at dressing a body," I replied.

Russell laughed, then took a sip of his cinnamon latte. The froth settled on his upper lip.

"Wait, you have something on your face. Let me help you."

I stood and walked to his side of the table and kissed it off.

"Here's to extra froth," Russell said with a satisfied smile, raising his cup in the air.

Suddenly a car sped past the window. A police car pulled out and followed, sirens blaring.

"I'll check it out when I get in," Russell said, turning off his walkie-talkie. "I have an emergency right here already. You need someone to walk you to work."

"Would you chase me if I ran?" I asked, reaching for his hand.

"Melody Shore, are you looking for trouble?"

"If it means you're the officer who rescues me in the end, then yes, I am."

"Get your purse. I'll walk you to work, Clutch." He put down a twenty on the table and we left.

When we reached the driveway of The Peaceful Rest Funeral Home, Alex and J.J. were hanging wreaths on the lampposts.

"Hey, look, Russell, it's Rudolph and Hermey," I called out.

"Funny, Melody, good one," the twin brothers called back.

"Why can't Alex and J.J. handle things tonight?" Russell asked. We walked up the front steps to the funeral home.

"Snugg promised me we would discuss a raise before the New Year. I don't want to give him any reason not to give me one. He's been so overworked lately. Alex and J.J. aren't pulling their weight."

"Those two? Have they ever?" Russell laughed. "But you deserve a raise, no matter what. You've what…saved Snugg's life like three times in less than a year?"

"True, and don't forget I solved four murders."

"Snugg couldn't do any of it without you," Russell agreed. "And who is laid out for tonight?"

"True that! Oh, tonight? We have this new client who is very particular about his arrangements." I wrapped my arms around him and inhaled his woodsy scent. "Do you want to come in?"

"Mel, this client can't be particular. He's dead."

"You know—I mean his family."

We walked in the main door and had to step around the massive pile of poinsettias and green swag garland that the florist had set inside.

The office phone rang.

"Wait here," I said to Russell as I stepped carefully around the florals into my fishbowl-sized, glass office.

The phone rang again but I couldn't find it, because someone had taken the liberty of depositing eight large cinnamon-scented pinecone-filled vases all over my desk. "Holy holiday," I muttered, as I tried to fix the stacks of files and search for my buried desk phone.

On the fifth ring, I found the cord, followed it to the console, then grabbed it somewhere around the seventh ring.

"Hello, Peaceful Rest Funeral Home and Cemetery," I answered breathlessly.

"So, there is someone alive there," a woman on the other end said.

"I apologize, it's a busy morning here. How can I help you?" I turned on my screen and entered the password.

"I'm calling about the gentleman you have laid out there, Douglas Freedmont."

"Yes, the viewing for Mr. Freedmont will be this evening, five to nine. Burial is tomorrow morning," I answered, opening our calendar. "Memorial information for Mr. Freedmont is on our website. Would you like the web address?"

"Tonight and tomorrow, everything about him is on the website," the caller hollered into the phone. In the background I could hear a man holler back, "I bet not everything. Doug had his secrets."

"You should know," the woman caller screamed back.

I signed off with the caller, then turned my attention to Russell, who was now standing in my office, holding a folder with a post-it on it that said "MELODY."

"This fell on the floor when you went for the phone." He handed the folder to me.

"It's Doug Freedmont's file. Snugg must have left it here for me." I shuffled through it.

"Wasn't a bad looking guy," Russell said picking up the photo of a smiling Douglas Freedmont. A distinguished man with a chiseled face, a full head of dark brown hair, and serious brown eyes stood in front of the red brick building that housed Pleasantview's local government offices.

"Try to make it in time for the couples' photo." Russell gently lifted my chin so I focused on him. "If you don't, my dispatcher, Joan Stoop, will seize the opportunity to try and fix me up with her daughter Becky again."

"Becky who?" I asked, my voice raising an octave.

"You remember, you met her the time she brought cookies to the station for Officer Appreciation Day. She's the redhead baker who owns Stoop's Confectionary Treats." He gave me a kiss on the lips before continuing. "She said I have great eyes. You sure you can't bail out of here early?"

"I wish. I already told Snugg I'd be here...what's the deal with this Becky anyways, Russell, Mr. Sexy Brown Eyes?"

"Very funny, Mel. I'll manage to keep the woman away somehow until you arrive." He collapsed into my one guest chair. "Becky is one good baker. Joan tells me every day that her bakeshop is thriving." He winked.

"Russell McCormick, you have yet to experience my chocolatier talents. My Almost-Famous Chocolate Chip Bars are to die for." I grabbed a pinecone from one of the vases on my desk and wound up like a softball pitcher throwing a fastball and fired it at him. "Now get out of here. I have decorating to do."

I spent the rest of the morning stringing green swag garland all over the lobby, including around the framed photos of Snugg's father and grandfather. After I had strung all the garland, I placed poinsettia plants and pinecone vases on the end tables throughout the funeral home. At eleven o'clock, I turned my attention to making sure the memorial cards for Douglas Freedmont were correct. Rose Freedmont had requested her husband's face on the front of the cards. He looked very much alive as the youthful, smiling Douglas. For the back she chose the poem "Don't Cry Because I'm Gone." I wandered around the lobby to make sure there was ample tissue and mints. I went down to the flower room, but it was empty.

Where are the flowers? "Alex! J.J.!" I hollered down the hall toward their frat room office. I can't have the whole funeral home decorated and no flowers for Mr. Freedmont in the Rose Room.

The Rose Room is the larger and most prestigious of our two viewing rooms with crystal floor lamps, large wingback chairs, and dark cherry-wood coffee tables.

"Grab some pedestals, and put them on each end of Doug Freedmont's coffin. I'll decorate them!" I shouted.

When I got no response, I ran upstairs to the Rose Room in a panic, only to find that inside the room, all the wreathes and vases of flowers had been placed already. There was no need to worry.

J.J. walked by with a giant bag of potato chips, a soda, and a gaming magazine. He plunked himself down in my guest chair. The tail of my office cat clock ticked to eleven thirty.

"How goes it, Mel? Want some of my lunch?"

"That's what you're eating for lunch? I'll pass," I said as my stomach growled in disapproval.

"Did I tell you Alex and I have dates this weekend?" He flipped through his magazine. "The 'Snowflake Sisters.'"

"Who are they, a singing group?" I asked.

"Two very talented chefs. They were both crowned 'Ms. Snowflake of Pleasantview.' It's the first time in the ten years of the pageant that two women won. I recorded their acceptance speeches on my phone. Which one do you want to hear first?" He began pressing the buttons on his phone.

"J.J., I don't have time to talk." I took the phone from his hand and clicked it off. "We're expecting a large crowd…"

"Why?"

"Who is the question! Mr. Freedmont."

"Never heard of 'm."

"Well, he is well-known in the community. He was the Public Works Director, and then Assistant to the Township Manager, and for the last few years, he was the Manager."

"A go-getter. Nothing to go after here. It's dead people every day," J.J. said, looking toward the framed photos of his family in the lobby. He opened his magazine, pulled a handful of chips out of the bag, and began to crunch on them.

Alex walked by carrying two jugs of formaldehyde.

"I'm a go-getter. Me right here," Alex said. He dropped the jugs and patted his chest.

"Yeah, Uncle A says it all the time. 'Go get this, go get that,'" J.J. chimed in.

"Not you, Douglas Freedmont," I said, showing him one of the memorial cards on my desk.

"That guy," Alex pointed toward Douglas Freedmont, laid out in the Rose Room in a bronze casket. "He used to be an actor."

"Douglas Freedmont? He was the Township Manager." I shook my head.

Alex grabbed their shared phone from J.J.'s hands and began typing.

"Says right here he starred in Cheater," Alex shouted.

"Alex sure knows his stuff." J.J. took the phone from his brother and waved it in front of my face. "Did you ever see that movie, Mel?"

"No, but I bet my ex could have won best actor."

"Hey, we might be able to score some autographs from his actor buddies," Alex said. "The guys at Mickey's happy hour tonight will be impressed."

"You won't have time. The viewing goes until nine p.m. You two aren't stranding your uncle again like yesterday."

"What do you mean?" J.J. asked.

"When that pipe busted in the cosmetic room, it shot water all over your uncle and Douglas Freedmont. It was me that calmed his wife, Rose Freedmont down. Snugg fixed the pipe and Mr. Freedmont's makeup."

"What would we do without you, Mel?" J.J. said as he held his chip bag out to me.

"I am hungry. But I'm not going to eat from your germy bag. Last week I stocked the fridge with healthy lunches for myself!" I pushed the chip bag away and neatly stacked the inventory sheets in front of me.

"You won't find much in the lunchroom. J.J. and I cleaned it yesterday. There were a lot of yogurts and cheese. All healthy foods. We took them home. Our dates this weekend are going to cook with a lot of superfoods." Alex patted his stomach.

"You guys owe me twenty dollars!" I stormed off to the kitchen.

In the kitchen, I was smothering jelly on a bagel that they missed in their clean-out with such force that it splashed on my cream blouse and stained it.

"I'm going home to eat lunch and change. Don't bother to get up." I hollered to Alex, who now sat in my office, his feet propped up on my desk, reading J.J.'s gaming magazine.

Outside, the temperature had dropped, and snow flurries swirled around me as I walked in my new snow leopard camo flats. It was a short ten-minute walk to my garage apartment on Pine Street. To calm down, I hummed along to pop holiday songs on my iPod. It had been such a great morning, no worries about groceries and a blouse.

My stomach growled loudly as I ran up the wooden steps. In the living room, my cat, Shady, lay on his sun-filled window perch.

"Protesting your name again, Shady?" I quickly changed my blouse and headed toward the kitchen.

Shady's eyes opened a slit as if to say, "Yes, this is what I do all day, now please don't disturb me."

When I moved in, the lease said no pets, but when this black and white kitten showed up in the yard, my landlord, John brought him to me. I was now a proud pet owner.

We decided even "tough girls" needed a kitten.

"I guess you don't want to join me in a turkey sandwich?" I asked Shady.

He didn't reply.

I made my standard extra pickle turkey sandwich and sat down at my table to eat when Shady wandered into the kitchen and straight to his treat container on the bottom of my wine cart. He meowed loudly.

"I really want to show Russell's dispatcher, Joan, and her daughter,

'Becky, the baker' that I have skills too. I'm going to show up at the party with something fantastic!" I said to Shady. I paced back and forth in front of my refrigerator. Shady rubbed up on a wine bottle. "Oh, wine. No, too quick and easy."

Next to the bar cart was my baking cupboard. I opened it and found an unopened bag of chocolate baking chips. If I hurried, I could whip up a batch of my Almost-Famous To-Die-For Chocolate Chip Bars for the party and be back to work in an hour.

I pulled my Gram's pink vinyl binder cookbook from its place of honor, front and center on my countertop cabinet. Inside were family and close friends' sought-after recipes printed out and preserved in plastic sleeves. Page eight had the well-worn recipe.

Forty-five minutes later, my house smelled heavenly of warm melting chocolate. Shady wove himself in and out of my legs as I taste-tested a bar and put the dishes in the dishwasher.

Once they cooled, I piled them three high on a plate, wrapped them in cellophane, and for a finishing festive touch, tied them with a bow left over from decorating Main Street.

"I'll show that Joan and her daughter, Becky 'The Baker.' They got nothing on me!"

Shady gave me an affirmative meow.

The jingle bells I had replaced our standard single door chime with gave a festive ring as I opened the door to the funeral home. I took one step and bumped into an angry Arthur Snugg stomping through the lobby like the Grinch. His purposeful steps nearly shook the poinsettia plants off the end tables.

"Melody," he said, spinning around to face me. His normally pressed suit coat sleeves were bunched up to his elbows and his white dress shirt had black streaks on it. His eyes were tired and his face was ashen. He raked his fingers through his jet-black hair and grumbled, "I am headed to the conference room to tell the caterer it is state funeral home policy that we cannot serve food."

Then he spotted my plate of chocolate chip bars.

"I'm running a funeral home, not a baking competition," he said through gritted teeth.

"What's wrong?" I asked.

"This is a three-ring circus around here. I need to get back downstairs to the morgue. The freezers aren't holding their temperature. I've been climbing in and out of the cooler chambers."

"I will go talk to the caterer. You have more pressing things to do." I gently guided him toward the lower-level stairs.

"Uncle A is on patrol," J.J. said as he appeared around the corner.

"J.J., you and Alex really need to help your uncle." I hung my double-breasted trench coat on the lobby coat rack.

"Mel, I didn't know we were having food delivered. I heard Uncle Arthur say it's not allowed. Can we eat it?" He pulled me away from the lobby and viewing rooms, down the hallway, past the bathroom and toward the conference room.

His eyes turned to the cookie plate in my hand.

"You brought some too. I've been eating all that healthy stuff at our apartment. I could use a snack." He sucked in his already flat stomach and pumped out his no-muscle chest.

"Absolutely not," I said, holding my cookies out of reach.

The large cherrywood table normally used for meetings with grieving families was now covered with boxes draped with ivory tablecloths, turning it into a display area on which sat various pedestal dishes and trays. The six chairs that usually surrounded the table were stacked in the corner. In the place of our standard coffee carafe sat two fancy beverage dispensers and a mouth-watering selection of cookies. A few pinecone-filled vases completed the setup.

Becky "The Baker" Stoop stood in the middle of it all. Her cinnamon-red hair was pulled up in a loose bun and strands hung down, softly framing her heart-shaped, smooth-complected face.

"Why is she here?" I whispered to Alex who had joined us in the hallway.

"Who cares? She brought food," they said in unison.

"She's the owner of Stoop's Confectionary Treats and the daughter of Russell's dispatcher," I said, motioning for the twins to go back toward the lobby.

"I'm more a Donut Heaven fan. It's my favorite. If the name alone doesn't make you believe in an afterlife, the donuts will," Alex said.

"Todd, that's not the proper way to lay them out," Becky said, rearranging her cookie trays.

"Todd...Todd Schultz," I said, walking into the conference room. "Melody Shore, Furry Friends Animal Rescue Shelter?"

"Melody, you remember me," Todd said, brushing his long, sandy colored, curly hair from in front of his face, revealing playful brown eyes.

"It's pretty hard to forget a guy who showed up at the shelter three weeks straight then adopted the oldest, scrappiest one. How is Tiger?"

"Tiger's pretty incredible. I've been so busy perfecting my new recipes, I need to spend more time with him."

"Todd, put the pastries I made closest to the serving plates." Becky Stoop pointed her professionally manicured finger at the table and then turned her attention fully on me. Her eyes traveled from my high collar, coffee-colored blouse down to my snow leopard flats, and back up.

"If you work at a shelter, what are you doing here?" she asked, turning her perky nose up.

"I work here at The Peaceful Rest, also," I answered.

"Boy, you sure picked two depressing careers."

"They're both very rewarding!" I blew out a breath. "And, because I am the assistant to Arthur Snugg, the owner of this funeral home, I am here to tell you, we cannot allow you to serve food. Who placed this order?"

"Rose Freedmont. Her and Doug have always supported us locals," said a man who rushed into the conference room. "John Schultz, from Schultz's Deli Delight," he said, stretching both his hands toward me. He was short with a stocky build and a grin that wrinkled his cheeks all the way to his smiling blue eyes. With his buzz-cut brown hair and fast actions, he reminded me of an army sergeant who had been told the war is over.

I quickly lay my cookie plate down before he grasped both my hands in his.

"I thought I would come by, you know, to set up my display."

"You came to check up on me, Dad," Todd said, locking eyes with John Schultz, who was at least six inches shorter. "Why are you here? Why can't you get over that I want to work with Becky and not at the deli anymore?"

John Schultz's eyes turned ice blue as he stared down Becky Stoop, and then he pulled me out into the hallway.

"My wife said to be professional. Doug Freedmont deserved the best. That's why I'm here, even if it kills me to see my son working for that girl." He turned and pointed towards some very expensive-looking trays stacked on the display setup. "Make sure Stoop doesn't think those trays are hers. I don't want Ms. Stoop thinking she can keep any of Schultz's Deli Delight's good sterling serving dishes." John Schultz then admitted, "They're not real sterling, but they sure look it and they have a nice solid weight to them."

"Mr. Schultz," I said, "as I was telling Ms. Stoop, you cannot serve food to visitors. It's against state regulations. You are going to pack up and get out of here."

John Schultz rushed back into the conference room and continued to organize his display. I stood outside the door, waiting. These people weren't leaving. Why were they here? Hopefully, Douglas Freemont's wife had not misinterpreted our meeting the other day. I said we are a full-service funeral home and that the cost of the service included the use of the conference room and anything she would need. Surely, she didn't think she could order food, and the funeral home would cover the cost?

"We have a problem," I said, reentering the conference room. I picked up a stack of cups.

"I'd get you a drink, Melody, but the beverage dispensers are empty," Todd said, his arms full of boxes.

"I'm sure she can get her own drink, Todd. We're done here for now—I'll meet you at the truck in a minute. I have to have a word with Ms. Shore." Becky Stoop yanked the cups from my hand and put them back on the table.

"Well, it's nice to meet you, Ms. Shore." John Schultz fixed a garnish on his overly huge deli tray, turned and hurried after Todd, leaving me and Becky Stoop alone in the food-a-palooza room.

"Ms. Stoop, funeral regulations dictate that we cannot serve food here at the Peaceful Rest."

"You don't serve my macarons, they are presented. My butter cream and lace cookies are sought-after pastries!" she said, her hands firmly planted on her size six hips.

Shocked, I headed back to my office to regroup, only to find another member of the Freedmont party: Rose Freedmont, the RD's wife.

"These were his favorite. I hope you can make sure he is wearing them." Rose Freedmont's vein-laced hands shook as she placed a set of cufflinks and a tie on my desk. "We were to celebrate our 45th wedding anniversary this year." She began to sniffle, so I handed her a tissue. She loudly blew her nose, then pulled out her compact and powdered her red, tearful face.

"Wow! That's monumental. My boyfriend is twenty-nine. I hope we get to spend forty-five years happily together." I pulled the picture of Russell on my desk closer.

"Doug was a good actor," Rose Freedmont said in a brittle voice.

"Mrs. Freedmont, we need to talk about the catering," I said gently, directing the conversation. "Mr. Snugg said we cannot allow you to serve food. I'm very sorry."

"Oh, nonsense. It's just some cookies and finger sandwiches. I'll tell Snugg myself, that worrywart. I've already paid for everything." Rose Freedmont patted my arm, reached across my desk for another tissue, and dabbed her eyes.

"He's busy right now, but I will tell him we spoke. He can call you?" I pulled a notepad out and readied my pen for her cell number. Instead of offering one, she turned and walked into the foyer.

I picked up the tie and cufflinks and followed her. She stopped at the doorway to the Rose Room which contained the casket of her beloved Douglas Freedmont.

"Please, go on in if you like. I will take these and have someone from our staff put them on your husband before the evening viewing. I'll be back in a few minutes."

The basement of the funeral home is a maze of doors and rooms. Some rooms I don't like to step into, and Alex and J.J.'s office is among them.

Alex bolted up in his chair when I opened the door to their office. His hand dropped a half-eaten cookie into a nearly full garbage can.

J.J, on the other hand, didn't hide the fact that he had taken a full plate of cookies from the upstairs display.

"You guys are pathetic. This room resembles a college frat house after an all-night party."

"Just a few empty pizza boxes, and we need these jackets and dress shirts," Alex said as he gathered them from around the room.

"How can you see in here?" I tried the switch of the only light in the room, a small desk light. It had one setting, dim. "I can't wait to see what happens when Becky Stoop comes back and sees you took some of her treats. I'll let her deal with you."

"Come on, Mel, you wouldn't do that to us. Besides, we only took one tray, and I covered everything back up. She will never know. These chocolate chip cookies are delicious. That Becky Stoop is some baker," J.J. said as he reached for another cookie from his full plate.

"My chocolate chip bars! I set them down with the caterer food."

"Calm down. Here, have one of these." J.J. held the plate out for me.

I raced back upstairs to the conference room.

"Quit trying to run my life," Todd grumbled.

"I think I know what's best," John Schultz answered.

Both of them turned toward me as I entered.

"I'm glad you're back. I need you to take down your displays."

"Everything's been paid for," Todd said as he brushed past me and toward the men's room.

John Schultz hurried down the hallway and out of the funeral home.

I looked over at the cookies. There sat my Almost-Famous To-Die-For Chocolate Chip Bars. They were now unwrapped and mixed in with the display for the evening.

My brilliant idea of baking to impress Russell was now incorporated with Becky Stoop's cookies.

At four thirty p.m., the Freedmont family arrived. By five, a parking spot could barely be found in the funeral home lot. The nearby Hometown Financial Bank lot was being used for overflow. I pulled out my notepad with the list I'd compiled of "Things to Discuss with Arthur Snugg at Raise Time," and added, "Establish overflow parking." I was already dreading Monday morning when the bank's manager would come over and threaten to tow the next funeral-home patron who used their lot.

Arthur Snugg walked through the lobby. He had changed into a custom-tailored black suit and his hair was neatly combed back.

"Mr. Snugg, I assume Rose Freedmont spoke to you," I said, walking over to him.

"No. Is there a problem?" he asked as he buttoned his suit coat and adjusted his silver tie.

"The food set up is still in the conference room?" I raised my eyebrows in question.

"I guess a little food won't hurt," he answered. "I myself missed lunch. But, Melody, you are going to have to restrict it to the Freedmont family. Also, no one is to carry food throughout the funeral home. This isn't cocktail hour," he said as he strode into the Rose Room to mingle.

"What am I, the food police now?" I said to the empty foyer.

I spent the next two hours trying in vain to keep people away from the conference room food display. It was useless. The conference room had turned into a mini buffet. They simply either said "Oh, okay," and then wandered back in after I walked away, or they laughed and said, "This food is compliments of Rose Freedmont."

Unable to control the party atmosphere that had transpired with the addition of food, I decided I could best help by offering comfort to the widow Freedmont dressed all in black, stoically sitting next to her husband's casket.

"Mrs. Freedmont, is there anything I can get you?" I asked, sitting down in the empty seat next to her. "I haven't seen you eat a thing."

"I'm much too upset to eat," she said in a tremulous voice. "This is the last time these people will enjoy themselves with Douglas." She got up and walked to the head of her husband's casket and firmly adjusted his tie.

I returned to my office. I needed a break from policing the mourners turned munchers. I was visualizing myself ripping a sandwich out of the hand of a petite woman with a beehive hairdo and green dotted dress as she paraded by on her way out the front door, when an older grey-haired gentleman rushed out of the Rose Room and into my office.

"Call 911, hurry!" He pointed at my phone console.

"What's wrong?"

A loud crash came from the Rose Room. A moment later, Arthur Snugg staggered out into the hallway, pulling loose his tie. Poinsettia petals speckled his hair.

"I don't feel very good," he said. "It's my stomach. I'm sorry, I got tangled up in your decorations."

"He collapsed into the flowers," J.J. said. He guided his uncle to a wingback chair and he and Alex stood ready on either side.

"I don't feel very good either," another man said.

People were milling around and I could hear conversations about the conference room food.

"Find out what he ate, I don't want any of that," said a woman loudly. She pulled winter gloves out of her jacket, put them on, and then carried her plate filled with sandwiches and cookies back into the Rose Room.

Fifteen minutes later, Russell arrived with two new rookie officers.

"Any time a 911 call is made, the police must show up too, even if the call is for an ambulance," he said with a nod.

"I'm sure it's a stomach bug or possibly my blood sugar," Arthur Snugg said before clutching his stomach in pain.

"He's been working really hard and hadn't eaten today," I told the woman paramedic as she took his blood pressure.

"I hate to tell you, but you're paler than the guy in the casket," she said to Arthur Snugg. "Let's take you to the hospital and run a few tests."

The paramedics wheeled him out to the waiting ambulance.

J.J. rushed over to us.

"Mel, there's a guy in the conference room, said he's the health inspector. Got a badge and everything." He held up his cupped hand as if he was showing me an invisible badge.

From the hallway, I can see "No Entry" tape strung across the conference room door and a tall, dark-haired man in a grey suit stood inside the room, filling plastic bags with food samples. He placed one of my Almost-Famous To-Die-For Chocolate Chip Bars in a bag and marked it.

The garbage cans overflowed next to me, normally empty except for a few tissues, water cups, and mint wrappers. As the mourners silently filed out of the funeral home, some gave me dirty looks–as if I'd called the police to put an end to their party. Others shot dagger eyes as they crammed their paper plates in the overflowing bins.

"Oh, Russell, this whole night was a disaster."

Saturday morning around six a.m., I awoke to a persistent loud knock on my door. Out my front window, I could see the two officers from last night.

I pulled my fleecy purple robe tightly around me as I peeked out my door.

"Can I help you, gentlemen?"

"Ms. Shore, we are here to ask you to please come down to the station with us for questioning."

"What? Now? Why?" My curious cat came to the door too, so I reached down and picked him up.

"The sergeant has some questions about last night's poisoning at the funeral home."

"Poisoning! What? Who? How?" I dropped Shady to the ground, and he let out an angry meow.

"You can ask all your questions down at the station, Melody. The sergeant wants you to come now if you can."

I made them wait while I fed Shady and texted Alex and J.J. a reminder that last night they had volunteered and promised to take care of Douglas Freedmont's nine a.m. service for their uncle. Then I followed the police officers outside. They offered to give me a ride to the station. I accepted and then immediately regretted it. I knew Russell's police car outside my apartment always drew attention, but when I walked out with an officer on each side of me and got into the back seat of a police cruiser, I saw the neighbor's blinds quickly draw closed. This wasn't a police boyfriend's visit. I was a suspect being taken for questioning.

Dark clouds hung low in the morning sky when we arrived at the undecorated one-story gray brick police station. Russell was nowhere in sight, but Todd, John Schultz, and a very unhappy Becky Stoop were there ahead of me. Todd and his dad sat with one seat between them. Becky paced across the tiled floor like a caged tiger, stopping with each pass to read the "STOP Police Personnel Only" sign that hung in front of the hallway to Russell's office.

I poured myself a cup of coffee and sat in the empty chair across from Todd and John.

"Do either of you know anything?" I asked.

"No." Todd's long, sandy-colored curly hair now had a serious case of bed head. He was dressed in loose black pajama pants and a T-shirt that said "Pastry chefs are rollin' in dough."

"My lawyer is on his way," John Schultz responded. Yesterday's friendly demeanor toward me had been replaced with a cold stare and grimace.

The steam from my black coffee brought me the only warmth in the room.

Down the long hallway, Russell walked.

"Ms. Shore, please come back into my office," he said before giving me a tight smile.

John Schultz placed a hand on his son's knee. Todd quickly pushed it away.

"Sure, talk to her first. The innocent will wait here," Becky Stoop shouted.

I turned a glaring look at her.

When we were alone in his office with the door shut, Russell relaxed.

"Mel, I'm so sorry to bring you into this, but we need answers. Someone put antifreeze on the food at the funeral home last night."

"Oh no! Is Snugg okay?"

"He almost died."

"He wasn't overworked, he was poisoned! I can't believe it!" I gasped. "Which food, Russell?" I began to pace back and forth in his office.

"Preliminary report says cookies were sprinkled with antifreeze."

"Cookies!" My brittle voice strained to continue. "Which ones? Who did this?"

"He is recovering, but they may have to remove some of his intestines."

"Oh my God!" I covered my face with my hands.

"Burned a hole through a portion of it." Russell picked up a tape recorder to start his questioning.

"That's crazy. Russell, you know I had nothing to do with this."

"I know, Mel, but we have to find out who did." Then he handed me a piece of paper.

"First, I need you to read this and sign it," he said, his eyes fixed on the paper and not me.

The paper stated in legal terms that I knew that what I said was being recorded and that everything I said was true, and if the law should require it, I would consent to a polygraph test.

I took the pen and shakily signed my signature.

He turned on the recorder.

"Melody Shore, please tell me everything you remember about last night, and you are aware this is being recorded."

"Yes."

"And I have your consent?"

"I just signed the paper, yes."

"Please tell me everything you remember from yesterday." Russell involuntarily let out a loud sigh.

I sat for a moment and thought about my day. Then I started from the beginning.

"I made you cookies."

"You made me cookies?" Russell grinned slightly and then the questioning continued. "What time was this?"

"I don't know, maybe noon or a little after."

"Where are those cookies now?" he asked.

"Someone mixed them in with the food in the conference room."

He hit stop on the recorder.

"Okay, don't tell me, let me guess...your Almost-Famous To-Die-For Chocolate Chip Bars?"

"Oh, Russell!" I put my head in my hands. He handed me a tissue and turned back on the recorder.

When I finished telling him everything that had happened, Russell asked my permission to shut off the recorder.

"Mel, in light of last night, I am going to be busy doing a little more digging on Douglas Freedmont." Russell wrote a few notes in his notebook and looked at his watch.

"Russell, I mean, surely everyone knows that I couldn't have anything to do with this horrible incident."

"Mel, it seems to me that someone wanted to make either The Peaceful Rest, Stoop's Confectionary Treats, or Schultz's Deli Delights look bad," he said. He closed his notebook and sighed. "I wish you hadn't taken the cookies meant for me to the funeral home. Arthur Snugg said he only ate a few cookies, nothing else." Russell's forehead wrinkled with concern, and he ran his fingers through his curly hair.

He escorted me out the back exit to the same waiting police cruiser, but not before saying, "I need to talk to the other suspects. But, please, leave this up to my department, Mel. Don't go looking for trouble. I don't want to arrest you for interfering with the investigation."

"Arrest me? Interfering…other suspects! Oh, Russell, you know I can't sit by and let someone poison Arthur Snugg and the spirit of The Peaceful Rest! I can't."

Returning home, I climbed back into bed. The first time we allow food in the funeral home, and Arthur Snugg is poisoned. This would be newsworthy for sure.

I had just rolled onto my stomach and put the pillow over my head to block out the world when my phone rang.

"Mom, I'm sleeping."

"Melody, I'm glad I got you before the police did. I just left Marsha's and people are talking about how you served poison food yesterday at Douglas Freedmont's funeral."

"I didn't serve or poison the food, Mom."

"I knew you wouldn't serve rotten food. I told everyone you're not the best cook, but you've never poisoned anyone."

"Thanks, Mom. I got to go."

"Did you read this month's self-help book I gave you? A Smile and a Cookie—Don't Leave Home Without Them? I turned down the pages and highlighted the parts where they talk about using them to your advantage."

"Bye, Mom."

"Melody, call me. They give you one phone call."

After the phone call from my mother, I couldn't sleep. I tossed and turned for almost two hours. When the clock ticked to ten thirty a.m., I decided lunch was in order, and I knew just the place—Schultz's Deli Delight.

Schultz's Deli Delight was halfway between my apartment and the funeral home. It was a short drive from Pine Street to Second Street. The dull and dismal clouds of the morning had given way, and the sun warmed the brisk December air up to a warm 48 degrees. I parked my jeep, Blue

Betty, directly in front of the store. A striped green and white logoed awning stretched the length of the storefront. On a large chalkboard sign the daily specials were neatly written. I read them and went in. Above the glass display cases filled to the brim with deli meats, cheeses, salads and canned homegrown goods, a smaller matching striped canvas awning hung. To the right of the awning, two large chalkboards listed today's sale prices.

"Good afternoon. How can I help you today?" said a platinum-haired, golden complexioned woman dressed in a form-fitting pink sweatsuit. She looked up at me with tired blue eyes as she filled the display case with Swiss cheese.

"I'll have the mini veggie sub with homemade Italian dressing." I took the sandwich and sat down at a small wooden table to eat.

"Would John Schultz be around?" I casually asked the woman after two bites.

"Sure, just a minute. Who can I say wants to see him?" She looked at the half-eaten sub and smiled kindly.

"Melody Shore. We met yesterday. I work at The Peaceful Rest."

"John, there is someone from the funeral home here to talk to you," she hollered toward the closed-off back of the store.

John Schultz, wearing an apron with the slogan "Deli Men Are a Cut Above the Rest," appeared from the back room. The door banged behind him.

"Your boyfriend already questioned me for twenty minutes and I almost missed the morning delivery. Now you show up here. I have work to do. I've decided I'm not saying anything else without my lawyer." He started to walk away.

"Mr. Schultz, wait, I don't think you had anything to do with this either."

"Well, what do you want, then? For all I know, you could be in cahoots with Stoop and trying to run me out of business by blaming the poisoning on my food." He stood next to the woman and put his arm around her.

"Think about it: It makes the funeral home look bad too. Arthur Snugg is like family to me. Why would I poison anyone?" I crossed my arms and then, realizing I looked defensive, I uncrossed them.

John Schultz stuck his hands in his pockets and paced back and forth.

"Well, what do you want then? I told the police everything I know."

"Is your son, Todd, here?"

"He's at home. Stoop fired him. You think he would come help here now."

"John, that is enough," Mrs. Schultz said. Her cheeks were now as pink as her sweatsuit. "My husband is telling you the truth–we didn't have anything to do with Arthur Snugg's poisoning. My money is on that Becky Stoop, too."

"Becky Stoop? Why do you say that?" I asked.

"When she hired Todd, John thought it was a bad idea. I told him it would be good for Todd. Now, I regret that."

"Why do you regret it?" I took another bite of my sandwich.

"Look at the mess she got him into. She's got us into. Making us look bad. We were doing a good business, now this." She took a cloth and began to vigorously wipe her counter.

I looked around. The deli was industrial clean. There were no other customers except me.

"Normally on a Saturday, we have people lined up waiting to get their fresh-sliced lunch meats and cheeses. We usually sell out of my homemade pickles, relishes, and salsas. But because of Stoop, no one today."

"That Becky Stoop is poison herself," John Schultz said. He turned and, without a goodbye, he left through the door he came out of.

Mrs. Schultz slammed a large ham down on her slicing machine and began slicing it with more force than a lumberjack. I thanked her for their time, to which she mumbled "sure."

Outside, I deposited the finished sub wrapper in the trash and walked down Second Street past the hardware store and straight into Stoop's Confectionary Treats.

Stoop's storefront was trimmed in white, and the large front window announced to all of Pleasantview it was the "OFFICIAL HOME TO THE WORLD'S BEST BAKED GOODS." A bell attached to the freshly painted white door signaled my presence. Stoop's was empty of customers as well. Assorted fancy cookies and mouth-watering chocolates filled the glass cases. The morning donut display brimmed with iced and cream-filled donuts. The smell of sugar sweetened the air. That is, until Becky Stoop appeared around the corner.

"What do you want? You got nerve showing up here after your funeral home made me look bad."

I took a deep breath and tried to remember the article in A Smile and
a Cookie: Don't Leave Home Without Them self-help book my mother
mentioned this morning. She had left it last week taped to Blue Betty's
windshield. Tip #1, take your smile wherever you go, and sweeten up the
sourest of people.

"Ms. Stoop, Becky, I'm here to offer help. I feel terrible about last
night. I want to find out who did this as much as you." I gave her a smile
that made my cheeks hurt.

"Help? You're a big help! You should feel terrible."

"Please, Becky, if you would just talk to me, maybe I can figure out
who did this. It can't hurt. Your mother and Russell are friends."

Becky looked around her calorie-laced bakery and softened like butter.

"I'm really upset. Todd quit."

"He quit?" John Schultz told me he was fired! "Why would he quit a
good thing?" I asked.

"Yeah, I know...ever since Todd started here three months ago, he
charmed my customers. Just last week someone asked for one of Todd's
melt-in-your-mouth macarons. That's my prized recipe." She gingerly
picked up a lemon macaron from her display case and put it in a countertop basket. On a tent card next to the basket, written in red marker
and underlined, it said, "Today's Special Free Treats made by the owner,
Becky."

"Todd is so nice," I said softly.

"I thought so too." Becky opened a refrigerated cooler and removed a
tray of pastry shells. "Maybe he was only using me to steal my recipes. I
can't believe I trusted him."

"Why do you think Todd and his dad don't get along?" I reached for
the lemon macaron.

"I don't know, maybe he tried to tell his dad how to run things." Becky
took the basket down from the counter before I could take the macaron
for a taste test.

"Were the Schultzes like this toward you before Todd started here?"

"Like what? We sell different things. His wife, Lynn used to come in
here, but I haven't seen her since Todd started. They don't understand
when baking is in your blood." She picked up a bag of icing and began to

fill the pastry shells.

"Did you know Douglas Freedmont well?"

"He used to come in here too, all the time. He and Lynn Schultz."

"Together?" I asked.

"Mostly. I guess they were all friends." She set down her icing bag, walked to her front window and looked out for any sign of customers walking down Second Street. A police car drove slowly by. "Wonder if that's Russell headed to play some air hockey," she said.

"Russell?" My hands began to clench and unclench.

"He was so funny last night at the party. I almost beat him until you called 911. When did you quit dating?"

"We still date!" My voice boomed through her store.

She ignored my answer and continued to stare longingly out the window.

Tip number two from Mom's self-help book—butter is not just for biscuits.

"Becky, your pastries are award-quality. You must have done a lot of events for the Freedmonts, then?"

"Of course, for Doug."

"Becky, I appreciate you talking to me. What do you recommend?" I surveyed the fully stocked donut case.

"I just decorated these gingerbread," she said, adjusting her apron and going back behind her counter. She reached into the display case and handed me a gingerbread cookie with a frowny face and x's for eyes. "Here, on the house."

After talking to the Schultzes and Becky Stoop, I went back to Blue Betty, started her up and cranked the heater. This afternoon's investigating had left me cold. I turned off the radio which was blaring my favorite 103 WROX rock music, and quietly bit the head off my cookie. I had to get to the bottom of this. From the center console, I pulled out a notepad and jotted down what I had learned:

1.   John Schultz and Lynn Schultz do not like Becky Stoop.

2.   Todd was becoming more popular at Stoop's than Becky—according to the story Becky told me.

3.   *The Freedmonts were friends with the Schultzes.*

4.   *Becky Stoop said Todd quit.*

5.   *Mr. and Mrs. Schultz said Todd was fired.*

I knew what I needed to do next. I needed to talk to Todd Schultz.

According to the latest address, the Schultz house was two blocks from their store on Second Street.

The house was a modest orange brick, ranch-style home with a breeze-way and attached garage. Large white pillars supported a small, covered porch and two small spruce trees on either side of the front porch sparked with snow. It was one of only six houses on a dead-end street. A lone brown Chevy Tahoe sat in the driveway.

I jumped out of Blue Betty and headed straight to the doorbell. A non-stop barking dog somewhere nearby alerted the neighborhood that I was on the Schultzes' front porch.

Todd opened the door before I could knock.

"Melody?"

"Todd, I'm sorry to bother you. I wanted to talk to you about what happened yesterday. I want to help. I know you couldn't have anything to do with this."

"Thanks, Melody, but how can you help?"

"Maybe if we go over it again." I pulled out my notepad.

"I already went over it with the cops."

"Did you tell Russell everything?"

"Yeah, he treated me like a criminal. Stupid police." That comment made me stop. How dare he talk like that about Russell.

"He's only doing his job. It's procedure, Todd."

"Well, he can stick his procedure."

"Todd, for him to help you, you have to work with him."

"So now you're saying I need help? Like I'm guilty." Todd's cheeks turned intensely red.

"I'm just trying to tell you…"

"You're just like everyone else, telling me what I can do and say."

"I'm not telling you what to do. I thought we were friends."

"I don't need friends like you!" He shoved his hands in his pockets. His eyebrows furrowed and his eyes stared me down.

"Friends like me? Todd, I heard Stoop fired you."

"I quit! It was a lame job anyway." He slammed the door shut.

As I climbed into my jeep, a pink Ford Focus car pulled into the Schultz driveway.

"What are you doing here? Stay away from my Todd or you'll be sorry," Mrs. Schultz screamed into Blue Betty's window, her hands fiercely grasping her pink sweatpants. She glared at me like a woman who has been told her over-priced designer purse is a knock-off.

I threw Blue Betty into gear and drove away. In my rearview mirror, I could see Lynn Schultz had been joined by Todd and they both stood side by side, hands on their hips, glaring down the road.

Boy, I really have ruffled some feathers. Someone has something to hide. But, is it Becky "The Baker" Stoop, or the angry, threatening Schultz family? I headed to the funeral home.

When I pulled into the parking lot at The Peaceful Rest, there were no cars except the hearse, which sat backed into a spot in the far corner of the lot. The snow we had gotten over the past few days had been cleared from the parking lot, but still lay wet and clumpy covering the grass. Stacked on the wraparound porch were overflowing boxes of the caterers' equipment. Alex and J.J. had double-handedly pulled off the burial this morning of Douglas Freedmont without a single phone call to me. Last night they assured me they would arrive early for the short service, and even thanked me several times for writing up a checklist in Arthur Snugg's absence. They must have read my list. Number ten, box up the caterers' equipment. But why did they leave it outside on the porch? It could rust in this weather.

"Hello." Nothing but silence greeted me as I entered the funeral home. On my desk lay the file of Douglas Freedmont with an attached note from Alex and J.J. "Mel, it was a great funeral. We're getting your checklist laminated. We left the caterers' stuff outside for easy pickup. A & J."

In the conference room, the cherrywood table had been cleared and reassembled with chairs surrounding it. The chairs that Alex and J.J. had placed in The Rose Room for the service were stacked neatly in the corner to be taken back downstairs. All the garbage cans had been emptied and the flowers had been removed. "Wait a minute..." I said to myself as I stared down at the photo of Douglas Freedmont on a left-behind memorial card. "John Schultz and his wife both have blue eyes! Todd has brown!"

I pulled out my phone and called Russell.

"I think Todd is Douglas Freedmont's son. Russell, meet me at the funeral home," I said before he could say hello.

"Melody, what? Don't tell me you're investigating on your own...this morning, you were on the suspect list, remember?" Russell sighed. "I will be there shortly."

I went outside to get some air while I waited.

Rose Freedmont stood in the parking lot dressed in a burgundy dress and jacket. She carried a black handle tote purse.

"Mrs. Freedmont? Did you forget something?" I gently asked as I walked down the porch steps toward her.

She rushed forward until her face was three inches from mine.

"Are we alone here?"

"Yes, yes, we are."

Rose Freedmont clasped her hands in front of her. Her head shook as her red-rimmed eyes stared at the empty parking lot.

"Oh, Mrs. Freedmont, I am so sorry about what happened yesterday. I hope you won't hold this against the funeral home."

"Oh, I will hold it against you, all right!"

"But you ordered the caterer," I stammered.

"You told your cop boyfriend that I came back to bring Doug his tie." She advanced at me, backing me up against the porch.

"You did. You gave it to me, and we put it on him," I said firmly. She was standing so close, my back pressed into the splintered wood of the porch decking.

"Well now, I'm going to give you something else. Tie up loose ends, so to speak." After that statement, she laughed a scary, disturbing laugh.

"Mrs. Freedmont, no one blames you for Arthur Snugg being poisoned."

"I'm the distraught widow. No one would suspect me until you."

"What? Until me?" Last night she was too distraught to eat. Suspect her? My mind was racing.

"You put poison in the food," I gulped.

"Just a little poison so those businesses would be ruined."

"You poisoned poor Mr. Snugg!"

"Snugg, whoever, I didn't care who ate it." She swayed back and forth.

"Why would you do such a thing?" My back bumped into the boxes of catering equipment, the cold steel of one of the fancy beverage dispensers wedged into my shoulder blades.

"They are the reason Doug had his heart attack. Favors for those people."

"What people?" I asked.

"The small businesses in Pleasantview," Rose Freedmont answered.

"What kind of favors did your husband do, Mrs. Freedmont?"

"My Douglas told me Lynn Schultz meant nothing–but I'm not stupid. You hear me? I'm not stupid!" she screamed.

"What about Becky Stoop?"

"I heard people talk how he was a regular at her little bakery. How sweet of him to stop for goodies for me. Well, you know what, I never saw a baked good from Stoop's store, ever!"

"So, you asked Schultz Deli Delights and Stoop's Confectionary Treats to cater. You set them up to take the blame," I said.

"John Schultz! He's an idiot. Didn't he see the resemblance between my Douglas and Todd?"

"They both have the same brown eyes," I said, looking down the road for any signs of Russell.

"I needed to make sure they all got what they deserved for ruining my marriage and my life." She produced a small pink pistol from her purse and pointed it at me. "Now you are going to get what you deserve."

"Mrs. Freedmont, you can't shoot me."

"Oh, yes, I can. With this small pistol at close range, you'll go down quick. But not here, your blood will stain the snow. Get up on the porch. Then I'll call the police. Tell them you asked me here." She backed away from me and paced the parking lot, waving the gun around. "You were worried about losing your job. When I got here, you were dead." She pulled a pen and small notebook from her purse. "Here, write your apology and admit to the poisoning."

"What?" I gasped. "I'm not going to admit to the poisoning. What's wrong with today's world? No one wants to take the blame for their actions. Even attempted murderers want to blame someone else."

I spun around and reached into one of the caterer's equipment boxes. Pulling John Schultz tray out of the box, I held it in front of me.

"That won't protect you," she said, swatting at it.

I dodged sideways and attempted to run up the porch steps. She grabbed at my leg and I lost my footing in the snow. Down I tumbled, taking Rose Freedmont with me. As we fell, she dropped her pistol. I grabbed it and attempted to stand again. Rose Freedmont stumbled to her feet and slammed down on my arm with her body. The gun fell from my hand into one of the boxes stacked on the porch. I fell to the ground again, pulling her with me, our arms and legs flailing about in the snow. We weren't making snow angels, however; we were wrestling and pummeling each other with clumps of snow. This woman was tough.

I was attempting to free myself from her grasp when my hand felt cold steel. John Schultz's tray. I picked the tray up and with all my strength, I brought it down on Rose Freedmont's head. She moaned loudly, her tight grasp loosened up, and her eyes closed. I had knocked her out.

A police car sped into the funeral home parking lot. Russell jumped from the cruiser and ran toward me.

"Now you show up," I said, collapsing into his outstretched arms.

"I am the officer rescuing you in the end...Although, it looks like you had it covered," he said as he surveyed the area and saw Rose Freedmont out cold in the snow.

"Russell, she poisoned Mr. Snugg! She admitted it to me and tried to kill me! Her pistol is in these boxes of caterer equipment." I rummaged through the boxes until I produced the pink pistol.

Rose Freedmont let out a whimper. Russell pulled out his cuffs, restrained her, and then took the dented tray from my shaking hand.

"One of John Schultz's irreplaceable trays," I said with a sniffle.

"Well, maybe all irreplaceable except this one. It looks like my girlfriend put a dent in this one."

"I guess you're going to have to keep it now for evidence." I collapsed onto the porch steps.

"Yeah, probably, or at least until you can fill it with your Almost-Famous To-Die-For Chocolate Chip Bars," Russell said, kissing the top of my head lightly.

Two weeks later, a fully-healed Arthur Snugg returned to the Peaceful Rest. A large "Welcome Back" banner sent by the Schultz family and Becky Stoop hung above the garland draped funeral home.

"Melody, let's have a meeting of the minds before the party," Snugg said as he walked through the flower-filled lobby and up the mahogany staircase into his office.

Armed with my "To Discuss" list, I entered Arthur Snugg's office. In his hands, he held a solid gray tie and a second tie covered in Santas.

"Melody," he said, dropping the ties and standing. "My sweet tooth almost cost me my life." Snugg's voice choked up as he continued, "I was afraid I would leave this world before telling you how important you are to me."

"Oh, Mr. Snugg, I'm so glad you are okay. I feel the same way."

"Thank you, Melody. Once again, your keen observation skills and detective work have saved me and The Peaceful Rest."

"Mr. Snugg, I believe I deserve a raise."

"Yes, Melody, you do."

"Unless you think I would be better off applying to the police academy?"

"I can't lose you to the police…well, except Russell." Snugg laughed and then picked up the Santa face tie and handed it to me. "What would I do without you?"

"Us too," J.J. said as he and Alex strolled into the room.

"I feel the same about you guys," I said, smiling at the twins, and then I added, "Most of the time."

Alex carried a small festively wrapped box. He laid it under the garland-decorated tree which I put in Arthur Snugg's office.

"Alex and I have big news," J.J. announced proudly. "Uncle A, we've decided to fully go after the mortuary science program again. We're both already signed up."

"Yeah, and this time, we will pass. Melody, we're counting on you to help us study," Alex added.

"You make us a family," J.J. said, clipping a candy cane striped bow tie onto his dress shirt, and handing a matching tie to Alex. "Cool idea, this ornament party we're having today, and the first annual GYHOP."

"GYHOP?" I asked.

"Yeah, the first annual 'Get Your Holiday on Pleasantview'" they answered in unison. "Your fall clean-up and decorate went over big."

"Well, maybe we can work on the name, but I'm glad it was a hit."

"We got the signup sheet for next year." Alex pulled a folded sheet of paper from his suit coat pocket.

"I didn't know there was a signup sheet." I peered over Alex's shoulder.

"It's not an official one. We made it. It was a great way to get some women's numbers," J.J. added.

"Let's call one of the numbers now, get a holiday date." Alex pulled out their shared phone.

I tore the list from his hands. "I will type this up and keep it for next year." I placed the folded paper in the pocket of my favorite red and black plaid holiday dress.

J.J. turned to Arthur Snugg.

"We got the numbers of a few older women for you too, Uncle A." J.J. winked at his uncle.

"I am proud of you both for handling Douglas Freedmont's funeral," Arthur Snugg said, "and I'm glad you boys are continuing your studies." Snugg patted both his nephews on their backs.

Russell sauntered into the room.

"No suspects here to arrest," Russell pulled me into his arms and kissed me.

My mother, Todd, and my best friend, Claire, peered around Snugg's office door.

"Can we join the party?" my mother asked, walking in with a platter of cookies, plates and napkins. "I made our family recipe for chocolate chip bars. They're not as good as when Melody makes them, but I'm learning." She began busily setting up a mini buffet in Arthur Snugg's office.

"I brought coffee," Todd said. He and Claire poured out eight steaming mugs. Todd turned to me. "I'm really sorry, Melody. I hope you can forgive me. It's been tough, but I'm working it out with my mom, dad, and Becky."

"Of course, Todd. Friends forgive." I gave him a hug.

J.J. picked up the small, wrapped box and handed it to me.

"Aw, you two are sweet!" I said, holding up a beautiful crystal snow-flake ornament.

Next, Claire handed me a red wrapped box.

"How perfect," I said, holding up a burgundy wool cloche hat from the 1920s.

"From me," Russell said, placing a small box in my hand. It was beautifully wrapped in gold paper and tied with a red bow. Inside the box was a vintage black lace-up boot ornament on a red velvet ribbon. A single key hung from the ribbon. A note in the box said, "You are the key to my heart—here's the key to my apartment."

"My girlfriend is a super sleuth who kicks butt," Russell said holding his mug of coffee up in the air to toast.

"And takes names!" I said, pulling from my pocket the list Alex and J.J. had collected. ☙

Melody's Italian Wedding Soup

❦

46 ounces chicken broth
14 ounces beef broth
3 carrots, chopped
3 ribs of celery, chopped
1 medium onion, chopped
2 pounds of endive—cook for 25 minutes, drain well, freeze. Chop while frozen

Put all the above ingredients into a large soup pot and bring to boil.
Simmer for 30 minutes.

Meatballs (small-marble size)
1 ½ pounds ground beef
¾ cups of dry breadcrumbs
1 egg
¾ cup of water
2 tablespoons of Parmesan cheese
Salt and pepper to taste

Bring the broth to boil again and drop the meatballs into broth one at a time.
Cook on low boil for 15 minutes.
Add desired amount of Pastina noodles (I use about 2 ounces so as not to soak
up all the broth after cooling) and cook for 5 minutes.

Gram's Almost-Famous
to-Die-For Chocolate Chip Bars

❧

3 tablespoons of margarine
3 tablespoons of Crisco shortening sticks
½ cup packed light brown sugar
¼ cup sugar
1 teaspoon vanilla extract
1 egg (beaten slightly)
1 ½ cups all-purpose flour
½ teaspoon of baking soda
¼ teaspoon of salt
8 ounces of your favorite semi-sweet morsels

Heat oven to 350 degrees. In a large bowl, cream margarine, shortening, brown sugar, sugar and vanilla until light and fluffy. Add egg and beat well. Combine flour, baking soda and salt.
Add both mixtures together and then add in morsels.
Spread in 11 x 7 brownie pan and bake for 12 minutes or until lightly browned. A quick sweet treat!

*These can also be made into cookies. If making cookies use 10 ounces of morsels. Bake 8-10 minutes. Makes two dozen cookies.

Acknowledgments

First and foremost, my editor, Polly Alice McCann, Alice Hixson, and the crew at Flying Ketchup Press. You expertly edited, coached, and brought "The Melody Shore Mysteries" to life. My family, for all you've done for me while I've worked on this book and for answering all my millennial questions. My Tuesday/Wednesday night critique group – Sally Hobart Alexander and the "hot tub honeys." No, they're not a singing group, they are a group of brilliant writers/authors who believed and cheered Melody on from the beginning. My "Sisters in Crime," whose wisdom and talent I stand in awe of. My beta readers, Paula Kurp and Donna Nardozi. You tirelessly read each of my stories and provide much needed comedy relief. Zoe Kennedy: You started my dream by inviting me to that first writing class so many years ago. My good friends, relatives, newsletter subscribers, and social media followers, who enthusiastically inquired about this book and patiently listened as I talked on and on. Everyone who took time to give me insight into the funeral home business; it was much appreciated. And you, the readers ~ Thank you all for allowing me to share with you "The Melody Shore Mysteries." I hope you enjoy reading this book as much as I enjoyed writing it.

About the Author

Carole Lynn Jones is the author of The Melody Shore Mysteries. To her, mystery writing is like solving a crime. You crack open the case, sleuth through the suspects then create a killer story– all while whistling in the dark. When she isn't writing mysteries, Carole spends her days and sometimes nights formatting legal documents for a large law firm in Pennsylvania. She enjoys spending time with her family, biking the many bike trails of Western Pennsylvania, and telling her cat Elvis to get off the keyboard. Carole, and her high school sweetheart/husband, live in a suburb of Pittsburgh. Find her online at www.carolelynnjones.com @CaroleJonesy on Twitter, @carole_lynn_jones Instagram

Book Design & Notes from the Editor

This book uses the font Garamond, a beautiful yet informal typeface. Its smooth curves and simple serifs have classical roman style form based on a cut by Jean Jannon, 1615, inspired by the designs from Claude Garamond in the 1500s, who took inspiration from Aldus Manutius in 1495. Alegreya, our title font, was one of 53 "Fonts of the Decade" at the ATypI Letter2 competition in 2011. Dancing Script is by Pablo Impallari, an Argentinian type designer based in Rosario, whose bouncing, lively font reminds us of Melody Shore.

Fonts, like good stories, inspire a long tradition of beauty and creativity and empowerment. The embellishments in this book were chosen with accessories inspired by Melody's takedown of a thief with only her shoe, a lipstick, and a compact. These stories are compact, but they share the tale of a woman who overcomes her fear of imperfection and loss and the death of her father to find her way home with heart and humor—a message we can all be inspired by in 2022.

This New Job's Murder was designed and edited by Polly Alice McCann in Kansas City, MO, for Flying Ketchup Press ® Carole Lynn Jones was the winner of our first Cozy Mystery Anthology Contest. In the words of one of our editors, the cozy mystery is for the reader a well-deserved day of rest and relaxation. We created this contest in honor of two remarkable sleuths and editors, Dr. Alice Hixson and Christa R. Miller. Thanks to Melinda Cordell for her invaluable editing and Kēvin Callahan for his inspiration in layout and design.

Made in the USA
Middletown, DE
18 July 2022